BOW   Bowen, John, 1924–
       Squeak

BOW   Bowen, John, 1924–
       Squeak

JUL 20   Z   491
AUG 8   Z   015
DATE FEB 16 BORROWER'S NAME   Z   029

Ⓢ THE BAKER & TAYLOR CO.

SQUEAK

by the same author

AFTER THE RAIN (play)

SQUEAK

JOHN BOWEN

The Viking Press   New York

Published in 1984 by The Viking Press
40 West 23rd Street, New York, N.Y. 10010

Library of Congress Cataloging in Publication Data
Bowen, John, 1924–
Squeak.
1. Pigeons—Fiction.   I. Title.
PR6052.O85S65   1984   823'.914   83-40251
ISBN 0-670-66617-3

Printed in the United States of America
Set in Plantin
Drawings by Eric Fraser

Contents

Publisher's Note

AS SQUEAK was born and bred in England, it seemed important to retain the British flavor of her story. American readers may, however, find some of Squeak's vocabulary perplexing, and we hope that the following short list of terms and their rough American equivalents will eliminate any confusion:

Weetabix	a shredded wheat breakfast cereal
crisps	potato chips
Complan	a formula from a popular diet plan
sellotape	Scotch tape
Petlita	pet litter
Cruft's Exhibitor	an exhibitor at Britain's prestigious National Dog Show
Smarties	M & M's
boot	car trunk
Do-It-Yourself	a handyman's hardware store

SQUEAK

ONE

Two Beginnings

I

It was dark and warm, and the world was small.

Once it had been a world of no limits. It was all around, part of her, and she part of it; she had been formed out of it. She had lain in it, motionless, and it had nourished her. She did not know, could not know, how long this period lasted, because she had had no sense of period, of any difference between 'now' and 'then'; it had all been 'now'. Now that 'now' had somehow become 'then'. The world was small, and growing smaller, very slowly pressing in on her from every side. Also she was hungry.

She had come to know that the pleasing warmth of the

world was not entirely constant. Every so often, and never for long, it became less warm. These times were marked for her, not only by the displeasing sensation of being less warm, but also by a change in the other almost constant condition of the world, which was a regular pulse, felt throughout it. From the interval between each beat of the pulse she had begun to derive a sense of time, and also she had come to notice that the pulse stopped just before the displeasing sensation of less warmth began, and that soon after it began again, the warmth was renewed. And as the world grew smaller, the pulse grew stronger.

She was hungry. The world now altogether lacked nourishment. Its boundaries were hard, and pressed from every side upon her body. Once, during the long-ago time of 'then', her body had been all of one nature. Now she was conscious that parts of it had different functions. In particular there was a part (it came to her) which had the function of breaking out of the world before it crushed her. The pulse was very strong now. It was an aspect of the warmth, which (she began to believe) came from outside the world, and would be even more pleasing if she could get closer to it. She began to attack the sky with her beak.

The first discovery was that the substance of the sky was much harder than her beak, which was pliable and not suited to battery. She became desperate, poking her soft beak blindly at the hard shell which enclosed this no longer comfortable world. She did not know, of course, that she was blind; since her eyes had never been open, she believed that darkness was the natural condition. She attacked on every front, thrusting upwards and sideways with her body, downwards with her feet, picking and poking with her soft and useless mouth, unable to understand why, when she had become convinced of what its use was, it refused to fulfil that use. She was tired and hungry, and grew more so during the struggle, but the desperation was on her to burst out of the shrinking world and join herself to the pulse and the warmth outside.

The pulse was stronger. 'Push!' it said. 'Strike! Break!' She did her best, and grew weaker.

There was so little room for effort; the world constrained her so. Her beak rested against the shell. Soon she must try again to use this flaccid member as a weapon of attack. Then she became aware that the beak itself was not actually touching the side of the world, but that there was a small, harder, perhaps sharper extension to the upper half of her beak, and it was this – yes, this. She tapped experimentally. Yes. No more thrashing about. This was it, her second discovery, the way she must go. Tap! tap! tap! finding every time exactly the same place. The beak had its use after all; it was she who had mistaken that use. It was a handle for the sharp point attached to it, behind which she must put the weight of her head, her whole body, not wildly thrashing about wasting precious energy, but exactly tap! and again tap! and tap! and tap! and on, until at last there was nothing to resist the point, but a small hole in the shell of the world, into which the beak might now be thrust, and turned, and turned, so that suddenly a whole piece of the world broke away, and soon her head was through, already deliciously nearer to the warmth and the pulse, and the shoulders, the wings could begin to work, and the world was crumbling, falling away into the past, and she had found a new world, as warm, but soft and large, of many textures (some hard, some squishy) beneath, but above it a boundless sky of soft down and in the midst of it the strong pulse which said, 'Home! Home! Home!'

11

She rested. But the hunger persisted. In the old world there had been nourishment on every side, and she had not even consciously fed on it, but somehow it had entered her. Then, when that world began to shrink, there had been less nourishment. She had sucked greedily at what remained, and had moved her head, searching for it, until there was no more. This new world, entirely pleasing to her as it was in every other way, seemed not to contain nourishment. She would move her head.

She moved her head upwards towards the downy sky, and opened her beak. The consequence of this was disproportionate to the smallness of the act. The sky moved; the world became at once much colder; the pulse retreated. She was alarmed. There was a sound, a high sound which expressed this alarm; it came from her beak; it was her own sound. She squeaked. Her body was agitated by alarm and guilt. Her wings flapped; her rump quivered. Then her beak was enclosed in another, much larger. The exterior beak opened wider, and her whole head entered yet a new world, a third world, warm and moist and replete with nourishment. She sucked in food. Her head was released. She gawped, and squeaked again. Again into the new world of food, and again released, and again the food, and again and again until she desired no more, and the squeaking stopped, and her wings were still. Then the soft sky settled above her again, and she heard again the steady beating of its heart, and, knowing herself to be completely happy, fell asleep.

She woke, moved, squeaked, and was fed. It would go on for ever. She was the mistress, this world at her command. If she wished for food, she had only to squeak to move the sky, and food would be provided. When she chose to remain silent, the sky returned, and warmed her.

Sometimes her body moved of itself, and a little soft stuff came out of her rump, and remained beneath her. This had not happened earlier, but it seemed a natural thing.

There was something to one side of her, different in kind both from the various substances of which the floor of the world was made and from the downy warmth above. It was smooth and curved. It partook of the general warmth and was warm in itself. She had no objection to it. She permitted it to remain.

She became aware, though without urgency, that there was still much to understand in her new environment, that there was an above beyond what was above and a beneath below what was beneath. She had to admit also the possibility that the sky had a dual nature, that sometimes it was replaced by another, similar but not identical. In her previous world, she had not, except for the steady, comforting pulse, been aware of sound. Now it was all about her, muffled for much of the time, to be sure, by one or other of the skies, but always there in the darkness. She did not make it, nor was it an extension of the heartbeat. If it provided food, it was not for her; it seemed indeed to have no useful function. Far below her there was an almost constant growling, of varying intensity, punctuated sometimes by sharper sounds – a blare, a warbling, a screech. A version of this growling could also be heard from above her, far far above; gradually she would become aware of it, then it would grow louder, then die away; this growling from above was never punctuated by other noises, being itself intermittent. In the air more immediately adjacent there were also noises, most of them occasional, as if objects or beings passed sometimes through the air, came for a while to rest, then moved on, and as if they called to each other, usually while at rest but sometimes while in motion. The very sky which covered her made noises, though not often, sometimes in warning or defiance, sometimes a calling noise. When this happened, she could feel the noise through the down of the sky. Once, after the warning noise, the sky had jerked violently, and there had been a sharp flapping sound, and a passing being had moved quickly away.

Sometimes the sounds took a concrete form. There was a persistent gusting sound which pushed cold air at her, which even leaked in beneath the canopy of the sky, and was extraordinarily unpleasant if the sky should be in process of change or removal. And there was a pattering sound, which threw liquid which was not food. Well, it would all be understood in time; there was no hurry. The smooth thing at her side, she discovered, was making a noise of its own.

Tap, tap, tap! It reminded her of something.

Tap! But that was over; that was 'then'. The smooth surface beside her shook from within; some living thing was there. Tap! tap! Then there was a small cracking sound; a process of disintegration had begun. Noises, a discordant jumble; movement, it was all happening at her side; the thing was obscene. She felt an agitation within her which later she would recognize as rage. She shat nervously. The balance of her comfortable world was being upset. The thing next to her was no longer hard and smooth. It was disgustingly soft, abominably warm. It flapped its wings; she felt them move against her own body. It squeaked. She was not alone. She became filled with the most complete and helpless anger.

Very well, she would exert her mastery, and move the sky. She squeaked, and was not fed. Panic displaced the rage. She squeaked again and again, agitating her wings, and opening her beak wide. The sound of her squeaking joined with the squeaking of the Other One; she felt her own wings flapping against the wings of the Other One. She was, in time, fed. So was the Other One. When both were filled, both silent, the same sky settled on both.

Time passed. There were certainly two skies, and sometimes the interval between their changing places was uncomfortably long. When this happened both she and the Other One squeaked, and were not fed. Cold was all around her then, and beat against her, and she would feel the quivering of the Other One as it pressed against her side, demanding food and warmth of *her*, who had none to give, and would give none if she had it. Then the sky would return, bringing food and warmth again. This world was not well managed, but she could still control it. She had only to squeak louder, to beat her wings harder.

The quality of the food changed, becoming lumpy instead of the smooth paste to which she had become accustomed. She ate it. There was a prickling irritation in her skin, as if stinging things were pushing their way through it from inside. After some time she noticed that the body of the Other One, as it pressed against her, had changed its nature and become grainy instead of smooth, though still soft.

Hitherto, the sky had attuned itself (if not always efficiently) to her needs, feeding her when she was ready for food and providing enough to satisfy the immediate need. But now began a time when there was not enough. Did it go to the Other One? She pushed the Other One away, squeaked and stretched her neck, but got no more, and since the Other One also squeaked, also pushed, the presumption must be that both were equally dissatisfied. A worse time followed when the sky remained in place above, and there was no food at all. Hunger grew in her. She made small squeaking noises under the canopy of the sky to remind it that there was more to being a sky than the mere provision of warmth. These squeaks were ignored. At last the sky did move. She opened her beak and squeaked louder than ever before, as did the Other One, the power of indignation in both being added to the power of hunger. Nothing. A clapping noise in the air. Nothing. Both squeaked, both exerted mastery over their world. Nothing. The sky did not return, they grew colder, and there was no food. They continued to squeak and to agitate their bodies until both were exhausted, and then fell silent, huddling against each other for warmth. Squeak opened her eyes.

What at first replaced the blinding darkness was a blinding light. She closed her eyes quickly to bring the darkness back, but knew now that there was light beyond it. Her eyes opened again, as it seemed of themselves, and she found the light less blinding and could begin to distinguish difference. Hunger and cold remained; now sight was added to them; she could not yet know if this was good or harmful. She regarded her surroundings. She was for the most part enclosed (which must be good), though there was space between herself and the dark stuff which enclosed her on both sides, and above and below. The light came from the front, which was open and composed entirely of space stretching out into the distance. She associated the light with cold, dark with warmth. Therefore she made an effort, turned herself completely round, and put the light behind her. A cold wind blew on her rump.

She had seen, and could still see, the Other One. It was living; that is to say, it contained movement as she herself did, and could in all probability move itself. Indeed, it had squeaked when she turned round, drawn away, and was

16

now attempting to make a contact. This disgusting object was of her own kind. Though it had moved to touch her side, it had not changed position, as she had, but still faced forwards. It lifted its head, and squeaked. The thought came to her that, if food were to be provided, it would not be by these dark, enclosing walls. She had made a mistake; the Other One was in a better position than she to receive food. She gathered her resolution, turned again, and faced the light.

So they lay together, facing outwards for food, but there was no food. After a while they ceased squeaking, she and the Other One, for it did no good, and they lacked strength to sustain it. Cold air blew against them; liquid was thrown in drops against them. She opened her beak to sup the liquid, but very little entered her mouth and there seemed to be no nourishment in it. Darkness came, not swiftly like the settling down of a warm sky, but gradually, and brought no warmth but only greater cold. Then there was light again, also gradually, and no surcease to pain. 'Then' and 'now' ran together again; there was no time but only an eternal hunger, like an animal inside her, growing inside her as once she had grown inside the world of the egg. It was a living thing, and would kill her to get out.

There was a noise, which came from somewhere beneath the floor of the dark box in which they lay. Shortly afterwards, a thing appeared at the front of the box. It was not a thing she had seen before, and seemed to be composed of various textures, mostly unfamiliar though there may have been feathers at the top. A part of it opened, and more noise was made. (This was, in fact, the sound of human speech, the words uttered being, 'Christ! There are a couple of squabs in here.' Though

17

Squeak was later to learn what humans were, she never understood the meaning of the noises they made.)

Since this thing in front of her was capable of movement, it might bring food. She felt the Other One stir beside her. She attempted to squeak, and failed. Well, it was over, then; all her mastery was quite gone, and the beast inside would break her open.

A light-pink object was extended before her: she saw that it was composed entirely of beaks. It lifted her. She was moved from the box through air. Noises of various sorts accompanied this process. She was set down upon a flat surface. It was warmer than where she had been, and the air was warmer. After some time the Other One was set beside her.

Noises of various sorts, not to be distinguished. There were two shapes which moved about the new space; she knew there were two, because sometimes both might be seen at once, on different sides and at different distances. The pink thing made of beaks had acquired a new beak and of a different colour, mostly shiny white, with which it touched her own beak. Could this be food? She lifted her head, and squeaked. The thing seemed to be trying to place itself inside her mouth. This was ridiculous, and altogether against the natural order. Food was obtained by placing one's beak within the larger beak of another being. Was the shiny thing attempting to command food from her, Squeak, who was herself almost altogether consumed by the hunger inside her? Weak as she was, she pecked angrily at it. It exuded something, a whiteish substance, a little of which found its way to the outside of her beak. Being on the outside, it remained there. Yet it was, she knew it was, what it could only be, food. It dropped away.

18

She saw it fall. The world had gone mad, and she would run mad with it, and then die.

Pink beaks grasped the side of her mouth, and forced her own beak open. The shiny white thing was placed within it, exuded more of the substance which was certainly food, and was withdrawn. Noises. (They were the words, 'Your bloody Weetabix has bunged up the dropper.') Several eternities passed, while the shapes moved about, but no more food was provided. Then the white beak was extended towards her again, her mouth forced open again in the same way, the white beak again inserted, and this time it exuded a warm liquid, changing colour as it did so to a shiny nothing. This happened several times, after which the Other One was subjected to the same mysterious process. The warm liquid was not food, not even as like food as the substance at first exuded, but it would do instead of food, at least for a while. Much of it, she noticed, had run out of the beak of the Other One. None had run from her own mouth. The Other One continued to squeak and to thrash about, but seemed unable to retain the white fluid. Well, there was the difference between them. Squeak, weak and bewildered as she was, held on to her determination to control the world. The Other One was clearly deficient in determination.

She was lifted again, and set down in the same place, but now the surface was soft. She felt the warm white liquid passing from her crop into the beast, hunger, which dwelt inside her. The beast became, to an extent, pacified. Beside her, the Other One squeaked, and shook, then fell silent.

The shapes moved away. Such shapes as remained were still. Suddenly there was darkness again, but it brought no cold with it; the air remained as warm as before. The Other One pressed against her. She could feel the life within it beating up and down against her side. Since this brought an additional warmth, she would endure the inconvenience. In any case, she was used to it; they had lain together so inside the dark cold box and beneath the downy sky. There were no more noises of any significance in this new dark, and it might be possible to sleep.

She slept, woke, and slept again. The darkness persisted. At some time within the dark, the Other One became still, and later cold. She moved away from it. It was no loss, since clearly it was a most inferior specimen of her kind. Superior specimens, like the shapes which had lifted her, opened her mouth and provided warmth, were much bigger.

II

Once upon a time, there were two Chinese Owls, one a red-chequer cock named Red Robin, the other a blue-chequer hen named Bluey. Chinese Owls are not members of the genus *strigiformes;* they are unrelated to any old horned fellow, sitting in the window of a deserted barn looking out for mice, but are a kind of pigeon, bred by the Fancy, close kin to African Owls and English Owls. Though they have the voices of pigeons and such pigeon characteristics as insatiable curiosity, a prodigal attitude to food expressed by scattering it, the puffing out of chests and strutting when asserting territorial claims, to which is added the dragging of the tail through dust when courting – though they behave, in fact, very much like any feral pigeon you may meet in Trafalgar Square, they do not much resemble such pigeons physically. Physically they more resemble Mr W. E. Gladstone during his period as

Chancellor of the Exchequer. They wear the same high wing collar, the same frilly shirt front, the same expression of indignant moral rectitude. They are also blessed with frilly pantaloons, and in this they cease to resemble Mr Gladstone at any stage of his long political career, unless we are to imagine him dressed in plush breeches which have been brushed the wrong way.

Red Robin and Bluey lived with other pigeons, many of whom were also Chinese Owls, in a loft in Warwickshire. This was not a pigeon loft in the usual sense (a wooden hut at the bottom of the garden): it was a bedroom at the top of the house, converted to their use. We need not here concern ourselves with the reasons for this. The story of how a smallish group of pigeons, some Fantails, some White Doves, took over a bedroom up to that time reserved for the use of the children of house guests (it had to do with a stoat, but there were ancillary complications), lies so far back in time and is so rambling that were we to embark on it the story of Squeak might never be done. Enough that our two Chinese Owls lived there with others of their kind until the day when they were put in a cardboard box and transported to South Kensington.

Many, many pigeons lived then as now in South Kensington, crowding its roofs and windowsills, and congregating wherever there is a kind heart to feed them bread or the comforting spill of garbage from the black bags which occupy the pavements outside the back doors of expensive restaurants. These pigeons are feral, many are diseased, the feet of many horribly mutilated. Attempts are made by public servants to restrict their numbers. These attempts fail, though often a hard winter will do what the Borough Council cannot. None of these pigeons is a Chinese Owl, a Black Lace Fantail, a Turbit or a Short-Faced Tumbler, or any other decorative breed. The pigeons of South Kensington are not decorative. It was to be the task of Red Robin and Bluey, decorative in themselves and the prospective parents of equally decorative descendants, to add this decorative element to the bird life of the Royal Borough.

Quarters had been prepared for them. A tea-chest had been begged from Whittard's, Importers of Fine Teas and Coffee in the Fulham Road, and the inside of it had been covered with black plastic to render it waterproof. This tea-chest had been placed on the flat roof above the door from kitchen to balcony of a fourth-floor flat. One side had been left open, facing the balcony, and this side was at first covered with wire netting, which could be opened from outside to allow the placement of food and water, grit and various nourishing minerals. Behind the netting Bluey and Red Robin would at first live for, if it were not there, they would attempt to fly back to Warwickshire, and having (unlike racing pigeons) very little sense of direction, would fail, to perish miserably in some outer suburb.

In any case, they had not been brought all the way from Warwickshire merely to fly back again. No, they were to start a dynasty in this new home high on the fourth floor, looking out over Onslow Square. One day, and that day not so very far in the future (when one considers how rapidly pigeons breed), the Chinese Owls of the Royal Borough would be famous, a tourist attraction. Open-topped buses would be chartered to tour Kensington's leafy squares and gardens, in which the Owls would roost, swooping in bright flashes of blue and red chequer through the trees, and from West Germany, Sweden, Texas and Japan the package tours would come, bringing the New Rich of the civilized world once more to old England's capital.

At first all went well, as at first all so often does. The wire netting would be removed when Bluey and Red Robin became accustomed to their new home, and Warwickshire was forgotten. Meanwhile they partook of food, grit and minerals, had their quarters cleaned once a week while they themselves were taken to the kitchen to bathe in a plastic bowl, seemed not to be disturbed by the noises of traffic below and intermittent aircraft above, gazed out at the balcony and other balconies, at roofs and spires. Rain blew in on them, but not to any greatly discomforting extent. Feral London pigeons landed sometimes on the balcony, and picked up grain scattered by Red Robin and Bluey from the abundant food in the dishes provided for them. As time went by, more and more feral pigeons became accustomed to the idea that there was grain for the taking on the balcony of Number Seven.

Then the wire netting was removed. It had achieved its purpose. Neither of the two Owls evinced any desire to leave the balcony, which instead they cautiously explored. Red Robin went further. He flew first to the roof, then to an adjacent windowsill, a distance of at least eight feet, returning exhausted for a nourishing snack of maize and maple peas. Meanwhile the feral pigeons had discovered that the prime source of grain at Number Seven was not the balcony itself, but a tea-chest on the roof above it.

It was true that there was already a pair of pigeons occupying the tea-chest, but they were smaller than even the most debilitated London pigeon, and in any case debilitated pigeons were not the first to make the discovery. The Owls could not be evicted, or at least not soon or easily. This was their home; they were brave enough and resolute enough, even strong enough to defend their tenure, but they could not prevent London pigeons from entering it. What was home to them was free lunch to the feral pigeons, who had homes of their own. Also, since Red Robin was unable to prevent it, Bluey was mounted from time to time in the easy way of the metropolis, in which casual sex is not a preliminary which necessarily leads to making a life together.

Bluey laid two eggs, one two days before the other, and the two Owls did what pigeons usually do, which is to take turns in sitting on them. Bluey sat by day, Red Robin by night, which is contrary to what the books say, but pigeons are contrary birds. For the feral pigeons, Bluey's motherhood was irrelevant to their main object in life, the searching out and consumption of food; they continued to raid the tea-chest. Bluey pecked at them, and sometimes flapped an angry wing, but could not leave the eggs. Red Robin grew ragged in his attempts to keep them out. He thrust out his chest and made proprietorial noises, he strutted, sometimes he ran at them. Mostly they ignored him. Even when the two Owls occupied the tea-chest together, facing front and striking out at any intruder within reach, the feral pigeons remained close by, perched on the edge of the balcony or the tub containing a dusty and ill-nourished azalea, watching and waiting, always ready to return, four heavy mature birds who had by now combined to keep away their fellows. Only when night fell would the Owls be left, Red Robin now on the eggs and Bluey beside him, to sit side by side in the tea-chest warming their eggs and each other.

It is possible that those of us who were bullied at school may unduly anthropomorphize this situation. It is possible that pigeons have no capacity for anticipation or foreboding and live merely from minute to minute; that Bluey and Red Robin were content enough to sleep side by side through the night; that dawn was not a fearful happening; and that anxiety and alarm began only when the first invader came out of the sky to land lumpishly on a window box, settle himself and thrust his head, snakelike, in their direction as if making some nice calculation of the number of wing beats required to take him to the tea-chest. Certainly the tenants of the top-floor flat were aware that their Owls were being harassed by London pigeons. They came frequently out on to the balcony to shout and wave their arms. Small plastic flower pots were thrown to no great effect, and one of earthenware, which broke. The feral pigeons would remove themselves lazily from the balcony to the adjacent roof, and wait there until the tenants went back indoors. One was shot with a borrowed air gun, and did not die quickly, causing remorse and guilt. His body was concealed in a dustbin, and the air gun returned to its owner. Within the same afternoon, the number of feral pigeons who had established rights in the balcony was back to four.

The tenants were accustomed to go away for the weekend: they had other pigeons in Warwickshire, some of whom had laid other eggs. During these periods an ample sufficiency of food and water would be left for Red Robin and Bluey. But what is an ample sufficiency for two pigeons may become less than ample when it is raided by feral pigeons. Some of the weekends were long. One in particular, for unexpected reasons, lasted from Thursday to Wednesday. During this long weekend Bluey's eggs hatched.

Pigeons feeding young require more food than pigeons feeding themselves alone: nestlings eat and grow prodigiously. Neither Red Robin nor Bluey knew how to search for food as London pigeons did. Discarded packets of crisps held no promise for them; they had not learned the goodness of Kentucky Fried Chicken spilled in gutters; even in hard times the dried vomit of a Saturday-night drunk, it was not food to them. All their lives, food had been provided – maple peas and maize, linseed, rape, tares, tic beans, glorious peanuts and the heady delight of hemp. In Warwickshire (if they remembered Warwickshire) food did not run out. In the tea-chest where, owing to the depredations of strangers, it did run out, more was provided, and they would scatter it, eat first what pleased them most, waste much, lose more to the predators, then await the dishes' replenishment. Now food ran out, and more was not provided.

They scavenged the balcony, but the feral pigeons had cleared it. Here and there with much endeavour, Red Robin might find a single grain, fallen behind a flower pot and already sprouting with the autumn rain, and he would eat it, and regurgitate it for the nestlings. It was not enough. Soon there was nothing. The nestlings squeaked, and were not fed. Water remained in the dish, and a slush of minerals, which nourished neither parents nor children. The feral pigeons had gone, since nothing remained to be eaten. There was no other course but that Red Robin should leave the balcony, and try what might lie beyond.

Daytime. Bluey warming the squeakers. Red Robin tried a short flight to the next building, where he found no food. (Much of this is conjecture; it cannot be known.) A return, then a longer flight still on the same level to the balcony across the street, then back to the tea-chest.

26

Nothing. Down perhaps to Onslow Gardens, on to the triangle at South Kensington Station, where feral pigeons congregate, awaiting the arrival of Kensington ladies with crumbs or squabbling over the discarded crusts of lunchtime sandwiches.

He was not large; he could not have been first in any queue. He may have found something – indeed, we know that he did for a reason which will appear. Whatever it was, the compulsion on pigeons is strong to feed their young; he must have tried to return with it. And discovered that he did not know his way back. He had travelled from one possible source of food to another, and now there were unfamiliar noises and scents all around, and a multitude of roofs and balconies; he could not tell one from another.

Bluey waited. She could not leave the nestlings, who must be kept warm even if she had no food for them. She could hear them squeaking, feel them squeaking; they asked continuously for food, and she had none for them or for herself. She sat on. It was past time for Red Robin to return and relieve her on the nest, then long past time, then her turn to sit again, and to be relieved, but he did not relieve her. At last, weak, hungry and confused, unable to fulfil the strong demand for food made on her by the nestlings, she herself left the tea-chest and the balcony. We cannot know whether she was looking for food or for her mate; it is probable that she herself did not know. She flew down to the street. She did not know either that the middle of the road is for cars and not for pigeons, and did not survive that lack of knowledge.

The two nestlings were left without warmth, without food, to be discovered by the returning tenants on Wednesday evening. They were taken from the tea-chest into the kitchen. An attempt was made to feed them on Weetabix crushed in warm milk from an eye dropper. This failed, but they were induced to take milk alone. They were left all night on the kitchen table, bedded down on an old shirt. During the night, one of them died.

Squeak lived.

TWO

Growing

In the morning, the Other One was found dead, but Squeak was alive and hungry. It was unlikely that milk by itself would provide enough nourishment for a bird who, since her eyes were open, must be nearly a week old. One tenant dressed and went out for Complan, while the other crushed and moistened more Weetabix. The eye dropper had clogged: something larger was needed. There was a bulb baster in one of the kitchen drawers; it was not often used, but had lived there for years hard by the garlic crusher and a slotted spoon. Using the bulb baster the tenant covered much of the kitchen table and most of

Squeak's body with a mixture of milk and Weetabix. It had become clear why the bulb baster was seldom used; it was an object altogether beyond control. The first tenant returned with Complan. *Dies irae, dies illa tremenda,* the Day of Judgement had arrived for the bulb baster. It was found unworthy, and cast into the dustbin; Abraham's bosom was not for it.

Squeak squeaked. Her Weetabixy wings flapped; her rump quivered. She could no longer move the sky, but she could make clear her immediate readiness for food and the duty of others to provide it. She had survived the night; she must be fed.

The tenants could not, must not allow her to die; it was a matter of human decency, and of pride, and of a duty owed to Bluey and Red Robin, who had gone (one could not know where, but it would not have been willingly), and had bequeathed this progeny, one of whom was already dead; if they were to have a memorial, it must be Squeak. The tenants engaged in a reasoned consideration of the problem of how to feed her. Would Complan and milk together do what milk alone could not, and if it could, would this mixture also be too thick to allow passage into Squeak by eye dropper? One of the tenants had fingers still messy with the Weetabix mixture. Squeak solved the problem by feeding herself.

It was really very simple. One had only to follow the natural order by which a beak is placed within a beak, a mouth within a mouth. The five pink beaks of the tenant's hand were near Squeak and, for whatever reason, they bent inwards, making an orifice sticky with milky Weetabix. Squeak thrust in her head, and banged her beak against the Weetabixy fingers, sucking inwards as she did so. It was not a convenient, or dainty or even quick way of feeding, but it worked.

The question of how had been answered; there remained the question of what. The two tenants had made a pretty poor showing up to now in the matter of populating South Kensington with Chinese Owls, but they were not ignorami. They had been keeping fancy pigeons for some time, had reared them and fed them and exhibited them in pigeon shows; they had won prizes with them. They had cleaned out their quarters, dipped them against lice, mended a broken leg with Sellotape and a toothpick. They had not themselves fed nestlings, since it is more usual to leave that to the parents, but they knew what fancy pigeons in general eat; Weetabix is not a preferred food.

The question was solved by logic. The natural food for Squeak must be what her parents would have given her. At a week old, the nestling eats food which has been first taken into the parents' gizzards, there broken up and moistened, and regurgitated into the nestling's mouth. The tenants lacked gizzards. They considered only for the shortest time the use of teeth, and settled on a pestle and mortar. There was still in the flat a large plastic bag of the small grains which had been supplied to Bluey and Red Robin and eaten, in the main, by feral pigeons. With these grains, crushed and moistened and supplemented by a little wheatgerm, Squeak was fed, at first in the way she had invented for herself, but soon, as she grew and appeared to be less fragile, by opening her mouth at each side with fingers, and shovelling the mixture in.

She ate, she slept, she shat abundantly. She adapted to the change in her circumstances. She could not be allowed to inhabit the kitchen indefinitely, for she would get no rest, and the tenants no food. A nest was made for her in the study, a covered cardboard box the bottom of which had been given a heavy application of sawdust-based Petlita (hygienically prepared and packaged in Romford). At night, since she still had very little in the way of fluff and feathers to cover her body, a convector heater would be turned on. Four times a day she would be taken from the box, placed on an old towel spread over the lap of a tenant, and fed.

She was not at first given a name; it evolved. The tenants referred to her as 'the squeaker', which is the generic name for all very young pigeons, then as 'Squeaker', finally as 'Squeak'. They believed her to be male, an easy mistake to make, since pigeons have no outwardly visible genitalia, and even adult pigeons are frequently in doubt about each others' gender. All squeakers seem to be male. They look like little old men in a geriatric ward, unblinking and angry.

There was no longer a sky; she had learned so much. The old interchangeable skies, which moved at her will, which were warm, which covered, fed and protected her, in which dwelt the heart beat that repeated 'Home! Home! Home!', they were gone. Instead there was up and down and all about. To see up she must move her head in that direction, the same for down. All about consisted of forward and back, and most of it could be seen for most of the time. There was a small part of back, just behind her head, which could not be seen (perhaps it did not exist), and a very small part of forward, just in front of her beak, which was much clearer than the rest of all about, and seemed to have a depth lacking in the rest.

Among these levels she was from time to time moved. Down was almost always nearer than up. Usually she was resting on it, and could feel its various textures, whereas up receded whenever she approached. All about was usually near, but out of touching, and usually of a uniform colour and either very dark or moderately so, but whenever she was lifted on the beaks of her parents, it was into a world of light, and all about receded also and came to be of various colours. Dark and near was resting; open and light was feeding. Only one constant remained from the long-ago, comfortable world of skies, which was that to get food, one squeaked, flapped wings, and waggled rump. It did not always work, but it was the only way.

Squeak herself did not regard the new method of feeding as being part of the natural order; it smacked of impropriety, and her attitude towards it was ambivalent. She required the food, but disliked the manner in which it was given. For the food she squeaked; against the manner she struggled. She would have preferred the old way she had herself discovered, in which her role was less passive, and food a commodity to be taken, not merely received, but she was not given the choice. The food was, however, no longer moistened. Moisture was added after feeding, by dipping her beak in water or in milk. In this circumstance she supped, she herself, Squeak; she did it. She did not control the dipping, but only she could sup up the liquid. It seemed to her that the ingestion of food should be more like this.

Soon, when she was held over a container of water, she dipped her own head. Soon she did not have to be held at all; water was placed close to her, and, if she herself chose, she dipped her head, and drank. If she did not choose, she walked away.

She walked. It was a new thing she could do. It did not seem new; it was just moving, which she could do before, except that hitherto movement had been confined to thrusting, quivering, turning, all in the one place, and now she was able to change that place for herself – not to go up or even (except accidentally) down, but considerably to extend the dimensions of all about.

It had happened thus. The beaks of her parents had lifted her, as had become usual, from the place in which she rested to the place where she was fed. Feeding had taken place, the usual humiliating and unnatural business, with water to follow. Then, instead of returning her to the resting place, the beaks had moved her on to a down of different texture, a roughness abrasive to the rump (it was a haircord carpet). This was clearly not a place for resting, being light, not dark, and also unfamiliar. Restless therefore, and finding the haircord uncomfortable, she had stood, squeaking, until the side of a beak had pushed her so that she was forced into motion, fell down, got up again, and walked.

Squeak was three weeks old. She had yellow down on her head and chest, bald patches of skin around her eyes and under her wings. The wings themselves were feathered; she would be a blue chequer like her mother. She ate voraciously, shat copiously, and squeaked persistently. She squeaked when she heard the first morning footfall of a tenant in the corridor outside her room, squeaked at feeding and to indicate that she would feed no more, squeaked at walking and at falling over. She had just begun to pick at tiny grains of millet and niger, offered to her at feeding time in the hand of a tenant; it was, as she had thought, the same principle as that of drinking, except that one had somehow to grasp the thing in one's beak and hold it still before sucking. She could walk, she could run, she was beginning to pick for herself, and soon she would be able to fly.

'A bucky little owl,' said the tenants. They consulted tables of nutritious foods and made up sausages of soya flour (46.1 per cent protein), linseed (36 per cent fat) and crushed lentils, which were pushed into the mouth of the protesting Squeak as a supplement to the evening meal. The tenants knew what they were at. Squeak would be a champion, and mated with champions, and he would sire champions.

So far there had been the feeding place and the resting place and the walking place, which was a downwards extension of the feeding place. The kitchen table, the tea-chest on the balcony, these no longer existed, nor had there ever been an Other One. In the whole world there were only Squeak and her parents, the two tenants, and even of the tenants there were large parts as yet unperceived by Squeak, who regarded the heads, shoulders and feet of the tenants as part of her general space, their laps as the feeding place, and only their hands, and particularly the fingers, as truly parental.

Twice her resting place had been moved while she was in it; she had felt the emptiness beneath it. Then what was beneath had become solid again, but quivered and bumped and had an unfamiliar smell about it, and although she had sensed her parents not too far away, they had paid no heed to her squeaking. This, which was the transfer by car of the cardboard box to Warwickshire for the weekend, had not yet greatly enlarged Squeak's perception of place, for it had involved no change in her way of life, which still consisted mainly of feeding and waiting, as any other squeaker of her age would have waited in the nest for food. But now she had reached the age of first mobility, when the nestlings of wild wood-pigeons tumble from inadequate constructions of twigs and baling wire to splatter on the pine needles, as from the dovecotes of country houses their cousins drop like manna to waiting cats, and even the ringed and pampered Selfs and Saddles of the Fancy scramble from nestbowls in pursuit of parents who are already looking for another place to lay. Now that she could walk, the tenants decided, the weather being sunny, that she should spend an afternoon on the patio, protected by their company against stoats and other predators.

It was a confusing afternoon. There was, to begin with, a great deal more up than ever before, and it receded into infinity. One could not know what enemies might inhabit such a vastness; Squeak preferred to spend much of the time pressed against the low wall which divided the patio from the drive, or under a chair, or, most secure of all, with broken spiderwebs and dried leaves between the wall and a wooden tub containing an azalea. From these havens she would from time to time be plucked irritably and placed on the lap of a tenant. The irritability was mutual; she and the tenant were both irritable, she at being taken from safety to a regular feeding place, and not fed, the tenant at the contrariness of a squeaker which, offered fresh air and sunshine, opted for the spidery dark.

Not only was the space itself unfamiliar; it was not her space. There were creatures in it. They came from up, moved for a while on and about the space, and would depart for up again, often all together on a sudden with a great whirring and clapping. While within the space, sometimes they picked at what appeared to be food, but which lay just anyhow instead of being gathered up in a dish or between beaks as food should be, and sometimes they strutted about, puffing themselves out, dragging a part of themselves against the ground, chasing each other

36

and making strange sounds. These things were not of her kind. They were not large enough; she could see all of them at once. They had beaks, but only one each, very small and of a poor colour, not at all resembling the healthy pink of her parents. Unprotected by a chair or an azalea tub, she was open to them. One in particular came several times towards her, made its nasty noise and would, she was sure, have attacked her had not her parents' beaks waved it away, and she herself retired to a more private place.

To and fro, new places and new spaces, but always the comforting familiarity of laps and the cardboard box. At five weeks she was almost completely covered with feathers; only a little yellow fluff on top of her head and a residual baldness beneath the wings persisted. She could feed herself now, was taken from her box in the morning to the lino tiles outside the kitchen, flapped her wings vigorously, and picked small grains either from a hand or a plastic food-container. The flapping of her wings sent many small grains skittering about the lino tiles, and these were by no means the first grains eaten; the tenants swept them up. Much of what was not scattered accidentally by wings would thereafter be scattered on purpose by Squeak herself, who had already developed the vexing pigeon way of aiming immediately for some favoured comestible and, with a sideways scything of the beak, scattering the rest of the food on offer to right and left.

She was curious. She extended her space. Even in the restful gloom of her box she would become bored, and squeak for entertainment. She took to wandering on pile carpets, and had to be excluded from rooms. Cardboard cases which had once contained *vin gris* from Haynes, Hanson and Clark of Kensington Church Street were arranged into walls to restrain her. She found ways of hopping over them. The cases were piled two high. Squeak's wings whirred like some agitated machinery. She rose two inches from the lino tiles, small grains whirling in her slipstream, and fell back in a maze of self-congratulation. Soon she would be over these boxes also. In the country she walked now more confidently on the patio, moving among the strange beings who visited it from above, inspected the grains they ate, and picked at some of the smaller grains herself until chased back to the safety of the tenants' feet, on to which she would climb, then up a leg, holding herself steady with a beating of wings, and so on to a lap to squeak for grains of hemp.

Her wing feathers were dark-blue chequers, her breast feathers light-blue. It was true that she had not yet developed the characteristic ruff and 'fancy pants' of a Chinese Owl, but at six weeks one would not really expect them – or no more than the merest indication. Perhaps, if one looked closely, there was an indication. She was gawky, ungainly, her head too large for her body, but at only six weeks. . . .

She could not fly in any real sense, but she could get over a wall of two cardboard cases by a sort of wing-powered jump. She could not fly, but she could get up on the side of a bath, thence to one of a pair of knees, rising like the twin peaks of Kanchenjunga from the scented foam, thence on to a stomach, and so over nipples or through pubic hair to the water to bathe herself. She could not fly, but she could launch herself like a rocket from ground to shoulder, there to cling and there to ride. The tenants decided that it was time they taught her to fly.

Flying could not be taught in London. It is not a hobby to be enjoyed in a top-floor flat, and Squeak could not be taken to Kensington Gardens or any unfamiliar place without the near certainty of losing her. Nor could flying instruction be given on the patio or anywhere too close to the Warwickshire house, in case the lessons should be too successful too soon, and Squeak find her way to the roof, there to remain in panic, terrified to make the journey down. This had already happened to two young White Fantails who had sat there throughout a day in August when chops might have been barbecued on the roof tiles. Neither the pitiful jet of a garden hosepipe nor the distracted calling of their parents had moved them, until at last, in the cool of evening, they had wandered close enough to an attic window to be caught by fishing-net. Not that for Squeak, the hand-reared Owl.

So she was taken on the shoulder of a tenant to the bottom of the garden, and placed on the top railing of the wooden fence. To her right, berberis and dogwood, potentilla and cotoneaster, rose and rugosa masked the septic tank; before her, leading towards the house, a lawn, then a wall with roses, a bed of wallflowers and lawn again; behind her a panoramic view of the agricultural Midlands. The tenant would retire a little from her, watched with interest by Squeak. Then the tenant would stand, facing her and holding out one or both arms, and calling 'Fly, Squeak! Fly!', while Squeak would decide in her own time whether and when to move from the fence to the more familiar perch of a shoulder or head. If she did not so decide, the tenant would come and get her, uttering reproaches which were to her as much mere noises as the earlier conjurations to fly. If she did decide to make the move she would be rewarded with hemp and returned to the fence, after which the tenant would take up a position further away. In this way did Squeak learn – not to fly, which came naturally to her, but to practise and extend this natural capacity so that she did not end friendless on a roof or in some unfamiliar tree. And, having practised, grew greatly to enjoy it.

Her voice changed. She acquired the two most basic pigeon noises: the first aggressive ('This is my territory', 'Put me down', 'How dare you!'), the second beseeching ('Come to me'), both prolonged. If she had also acquired the considerably shorter, frightened third ('Oh God! Trouble!'), she had no occasion to use it. She could not yet be put into the attic loft with the other pigeons, for they would bully a strange squab. They had been known to kill squeakers which had strayed from their nestbowls out of the immediate protection of parents, and although Squeak, at seven weeks, would be a less vulnerable victim, squabs of her age, thought to be pushy or merely over-eager for food, had been scalped in that loft by their elders. Many breeders have a partitioned area, the Young Bird Loft, in which young birds may live together in comparative amity, but there was none such in the attic.

The tenants did not yet know that Squeak did not consider the pigeons of the attic loft to be creatures of her own kind, and were looking forward to the time when they could leave her there; it was not good for her to spend so much of her life in a cardboard box, as in London she must. She had developed the habit of calling to them insistently, uninterruptedly, at 8.30 in the morning, which was the time she believed they should get out of bed and although they did not share this belief, it became simpler to let Squeak have her way. Removed from her box, she would exercise her wings vigorously from a standing position before taking a light snack on the lino tiles, thereafter joining the tenants for breakfast, when she might attempt to pick the rounder characters from any typed sheets of paper in the morning mail, or sport with paper clips, or, should she find the mail uninteresting, simply sit contentedly on foot or shoulder until it was time to wash the dishes, when she might have to be prevented from taking a bath.

So far a full life, but then the tenants were likely, in London, to go out into the world, and she could not go with them, nor be given the run of the flat without fouling it. In Warwickshire they went out less, and she had the patio, the garden, even the roof, which she could now reach and from it descend. Indoors the kitchen floor was of quarry tiles, the living-room floor of wood, and she was allowed the freedom of these. She developed an attachment to a piece of bronze sculpture, *Harbinger Bird IV* by Elizabeth Frink, and would perch on it for long periods, needing no other company, surveying her territory. She had many territories at this time, and maintained claim to them all.

At about this time Red Robin returned. The tea-chest had never been removed from its place above the door to the balcony. One evening, the weather being mild, the tenants went out on the balcony, and found him in his old place, fierce and thin. He was given food and water and, when night fell, caught, for it is easy to catch pigeons in the dark, as night predators know. Since it had to be assumed that he had spent eight weeks more or less in the company of feral pigeons, who are known to be infested with parasites, he was not allowed to associate with Squeak, but isolated in a cardboard box of his own, and in the morning dipped and dusted against lice. There is a liquid, imported from Holland at three pounds for a small bottle, warranted only to kill bacteria in drinking water but believed by the Fancy to destroy all internal parasites and cure most diseases. This was added both to Red Robin's drinking water and to Squeak's, and by the weekend it was considered safe to allow them to travel together. Placed together in the one box, they recognized no kinship, but fought with cries of rage and a vicious flapping of wings until separated again. In the fracas Squeak, at nine weeks old, gave as good as she got, confirming the tenants' belief that she was male. As for Red Robin, once returned to the attic loft, he found himself another blue-chequer hen, settled into domesticity, and no longer plays any major part in this story.

Clearly Squeak could defend herself. There was no longer any reason against introducing her into the loft. She would be able to find a perch for herself, and defend it. She would share the food and water. She was already used to the roof, and had only to make the connection between it and the window leading indoors. Her London days must now be over. She would make new friends (though friendship is not an art much practised among pigeons), would find a mate, become part of the life of the community. The tenants were no longer sure that she was a champion to sire champions; she seemed, in fact, distinctly underfeathered. But no doubt she would do well enough.

Not all the pigeons in the loft were Chinese Owls, though most were, since only the Owls were bred for show. The earliest acquisitions had been of other breeds – White Doves and Fantails, a Tippler, some Muffed Tumblers, and Saxon Shields, picked up haphazardly. Most of these older birds had names. There was Barbara

Cartland (who later became egg-bound, and died of it) and her daughter, Lady Lewisham, a greedy bird who would have grown fat if she had not been forever anxiously running about, convinced that there were sources of food known to the others but concealed from her. There were Mr and Mrs Carpet Slippers, a pair of Muffed Tumblers who, after living in amity for three years, divorced each other without any enforced separation when Mr Carpet Slippers cohabited with their own daughter, Squabby Carpet Slippers, and Mrs Carpet Slippers took up with Speck Two, a high flier and king of the loft. There were Wilf and Wendell, Short-Faced Tumblers, a gay couple, who had gone through life as Wilf and Wendy until it was observed that they took it in turns to assume the dominant position when mating, and now lived together very lovingly, and never laid eggs. Most of the Chinese Owls had not been given names, since there were too many of them, and the different varieties looked alike, so that even Red Robin had already become Red Robin One to differentiate him from Red Robins Two and Three. Later some Owls were hand-reared, and did therefore acquire names, but at this time the only distinctively named Owl was Ginge, a magnificent Cream, who had trouble with his fertility, but went on to win three Certificates and become the longed-for champion.

Back in Kensington, the tenants took to sleeping in of a morning. When they returned to Warwickshire on the Friday, Squeak was waiting at the window of the attic loft. The car stopped, doors opened, briefcases and carrier bags of food were removed, and already she was down, landing clumsily on a head, and clutching skin and hair with her claws to keep her balance. She showed no disposition to return to the loft for the rest of the day, nor

43

was she required to do so. Taken there at night, she evicted a young Owl from a perch near the door, and settled. In the morning she was at the window again.

One of the tenants said, 'I thought I might take her for a walk this afternoon.'

The other said, 'She's not very Owlish, is she?'

As long as they had been in her company day by day (and knowing, as they thought, her parentage), it had been possible for the tenants to allow their minds to slide over a lack of owlishness in her appearance, as a fond mother will describe a child with brain damage as 'a slow developer'. But this bird which had watched for them so long from an attic window and now came swooping down to claim them, was not a Chinese Owl. She had no hint of a ruff, no fancy pants, no frill of feathers on her chest. Gawky and ill-proportioned as she still was, it could plainly be seen what she would become – a London Streeter, own kin to the feral birds of the metropolis. Oh, perhaps she would be a little smaller than the common run, for certainly a Chinese Owl had been her mother; feral pigeons are not cuckoos, to slip eggs secretly into the nests of foster parents. During those few weeks on the balcony when the wire netting had been removed from the tea-chest Bluey had been well covered by visitors, casually but thoroughly, and certainly often, and the genes of feral pigeons are potent. Pour into the genetic pool what fancy mixes you may, it all comes out Cockney.

However, she was theirs. They had saved her; they had reared her; they were responsible for her. They had never owned a dog. Both dogs and doves had seemed appropriate to a country cottage (both being almost equally inappropriate to domestic life in South Kensington, though dogs abound there), but the doves had come first, and had precluded dogs. Squeak's behaviour at this moment seemed to the tenants more doglike than dovelike. They would, therefore, take her for a walk across the fields.

Once hawks were loosed from the wrists of men on horses. They were loosed, they hunted, they returned. The tenants had no horse, and Squeak would not be required to hunt; in other respects, the principle was the same. Squeak's preferred perch was a shoulder, not a wrist, and she went untethered. After some while she found the motion uncomfortable. To ride the shoulder of a tenant in Wellington boots, who is walking across the modern remains of a medieval open-field system, must be in some respects like riding a camel. She rose in the air, and circled above the tenants.

At first they watched her in some alarm. Would she come back? – it is always the question with pigeons. Was this the sudden disoriented flight of a pigeon in panic, or merely a statement of independence? If the first, then she herself would not know where she was going, would fly until she tired, then settle in unfamiliar country to starve or be picked off by predators. If the second, they might have a long wait beneath a tree. They watched her fly to the south-west. Should they run after her? It would do no good. At the far edge of the field, she began to turn anti-clockwise. Yes, she was circling round the field to the woods at the north side, then on east towards the house, then back in another circle smaller than the first, and so again, always in smaller circles, until she had exercised enough, and returned to make a clumsy landing on a head. So it went for the rest of the walk, over two fields, along a bridle path, through woods, and back down the private road to the house. Only through the woods, where she might not be able to see them so easily if she flew up, was she tucked inside a shirt. For the rest, she flew or rode as she pleased.

For Squeak the matter was at first simple. She flew, and returned home; that is what pigeons do. Home was where her parents were; that is where she lived. The concepts of Kensington and Warwickshire, of flat and car and house, were equally unfamiliar to her. Insofar as she recognized them, they were backgrounds to the shoulders and heads which formed safe perches, owned by Squeak, and the five-beaked hands which held and fed her.

She flew. She felt the wind in her feathers, and heard it singing. She played with it, gliding on it, cracking it between her wings. She looked down. Trees, hedges, sheep and cows, the fields like green corrugated iron, gates and fences, she had the mastery of them all, and there in the midst of them, her two points of reference. On that first walk she returned always to them. But later, since it is not always easy to settle on a moving perch, she would land at a little distance, and wait until one came to her, to carry her a while until she should decide to fly again.

The tenants were delighted. 'We take our pigeon for a walk,' they said. Foolish to believe so. Doves are not dogs. It is doubtful whether Squeak ever knew that 'going for a walk' was what she was doing. Certainly she never scratched at the door, whined, jumped up and down, used any of her restricted pigeon vocabulary to indicate that she was eager for such a treat. She enjoyed flying, but did not require to be carried into the middle of a field to do so; she could fly very well from the roof. Moreover there was an inequality of effort in this going for a walk. Each time Squeak took off she would fly in circles for nearly a mile. The tenants meanwhile walked less than a hundred yards.

By the end of a walk of (for the tenants) only moderate duration, Squeak would have tired of flying, nor did she find either emotional satisfaction or physical comfort in being carried inside a shirt.

There was also an episode with an actual dog on an actual walk in the company of a tweed hat, which (the dog, not the hat) had jumped up at her and frightened her. It frightened the tenants also, since the dog's jaws snapped within six inches of Squeak, and there was a sharp request to the man in the tweed hat to get his dog away before she came down again. More and more, as Squeak grew used to living in the attic, it was the roof of the house which began to seem to her a fixed and far more stable point of reference. Let her parents wander as they wished about fields and woods. She was a young bird now, her own mistress. Ties of parenthood must be broken; it was past time for the tenants to lay again, though they showed no signs of doing so. Taken for a walk one Sunday morning, she rose as usual from a shoulder, circled once, twice, then returned to the roof. When the tenants came back across the fields half an hour later, she was waiting for them, flew down from the roof, and rode with them for the last twenty yards of the walk.

Pigeon parents drive out a nestling long before it reaches Squeak's age. Her relationship with the tenants had become false, though neither she nor they knew it. To her they still represented security, a source of food and, perhaps above all, kinship. She lived among the pigeons of the loft, ate and drank with them during the tenants' absence, disputed territory with them, reached accommodations with them, but would have done so with any beings of any kind which allowed her the same freedom. It happened that only other pigeons would, but she could not know that. As for the tenants, Squeak was quite simply theirs, by right of salvation. They had saved her from death; she was their special bird. It seemed natural to them that she should watch for them, and wish to share their company.

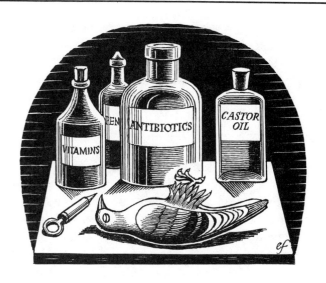

THREE

Deaths and Entrances

BARBARA CARTLAND died soon after Squeak came to live permanently in the loft. She was a Saxon Shield, one of a pair, her own shield yellow, her mate's red, and she was further distinguished by a white crest, which he lacked. Saxon Shields are large and clumsy birds, but Barbara, though she was of a full figure, possessed a certain elegance, particularly in repose.

What one does best is often what one most prefers to do. It was so for Barbara; repose suited her, and she preferred repose. Her mate, Mr Saxon, was not at all reposeful. He fussed. It is probable that theirs had been a forced pairing, one of those arbitrary matches made at shows, when a buyer places birds from two different breeders together in a cardboard box, and hopes for romance. The same sort of arrangement, one gathers, is common among the landed aristocracy, and often works very well. For Barbara and Mr Saxon it did not.

Mr Saxon was large and stupid and round of body. One could imagine a small moustache beneath his beak; one could imagine him at ease with his fellows in the wine bars of the City of London; one could imagine him, puffed out in a red jacket, at dinner with some Worshipful Company. He knew his duty, which was to produce issue, and his way of setting about it was the pigeon equivalent of, 'Come along, old girl. Might as well get it over.' It was an approach certain to ruffle the sensibilities of an elegant lady in repose, and it did. Sometimes Barbara would shrink away, sometimes she would strike at him languidly; once she lost tail feathers attempting to escape through wire. They never mated and were after a while separated, he to pair with a Tumbler and produce two sons, Bully Boys One and Two, birds so repellent of aspect and temperament as to ensure that all the eggs he fertilized thereafter could not be allowed to hatch; she to find a partner of her own choice, a devoted (and younger) Fantail by whom she had one daughter, Lady Lewisham, and then no more. Sometimes the Fantail would try to drive her to a nest, but she did not take to it, did not seem even to understand what he was about, and he had too much respect for her to persist.

When the tenants were in residence, which that summer they were for long periods, food was not provided inside the loft. The pigeons were expected to show themselves and eat *al fresco*. Twice or three times a day grain would be scattered on the patio. Those pigeons on the roof would fly down for it. Those in the loft, apprised of what was happening (for there would always be one on watch at the window), would come scurrying out to join them. Serene among them, like a Zeppelin among Tiger Moths, would be Barbara, who had the strongest partiality to grub. Her full figure grew fuller, though always in proportion.

The pigeons flew down also for baths, which were taken in their own time in two plastic bowls, permanently on the patio, kept full of water to which salt and a little glycerine had been added; the water was changed daily. In this activity also, Barbara joined them. She was never the first to bathe, and would not willingly share a bowl except with the Fantail. When the communal splashing and bickering was over, she would heave herself to the plastic edge, stand there for a while contemplating what was to come, make a little jump, and lie semi-submerged in the ripples while he first stood guard, then cautiously joined her. Watching her lying afterwards in the sun, rolled partly over on to her side with one wing held in the air to dry it, the tenants remarked that she might have been painted by Rubens.

Then one day, scurrying down for food, she landed badly among bearded irises and remained there, bewildered and winded. After a while she removed to the patio, but it was observed that she seemed to have lost her appetite, picked a little then wandered away from the food, but made no attempt to fly back up to the loft.

However, it was not unusual on a sunny day for a bird known to abhor all forms of energetic display to spend time at ground level. It was not encouraged; the tenants still feared the stoat (later that year to be discovered climbing wisteria in an attempt to reach the roof, and shot, with breakage to a first-floor window). But on a summer afternoon, when the tenants were in and out, seldom both leaving the patio for more than a few minutes, there seemed to be no great harm in it. Barbara remained, largely unnoticed, in a patch of sunlight, moving with it, until early evening.

The last feed was done. The pigeons flew up, some to return indoors, some to strut for a while on the coping or flutter between windows or take off in sudden flight. Those who were hatching eggs took the places of their partners on the day shift who in turn emerged for a sniff of the evening air and a short constitutional. Barbara remained, though the patch of sunlight was now well beyond her. One of the tenants said, 'There's something wrong with that bird.'

From the roof the young Fantail was calling her. She raised her head, but did not reply. He flew down to the top of the bird table and called again. She stood, walked heavily across the patio, then fluttered back up to the flower bed into which she had earlier fallen. The Fantail joined her and caressed her neck.

It was clear that she could not fly from the ground to the roof. One tenant stood up. 'I'd better get her in.' The other restrained him. 'Let him do it.'

The flower bed was in two terraces, one four feet higher than the other. The Fantail flew to the higher bed, and called again. Barbara took a few steps, and sat down. He flew back to her, caressed her again, then returned to the upper bed and called her. No longer serene or elegant, the effort manifest, she achieved the upper flower bed. The Fantail sat with her for a while, side by side. She inclined her beak towards him, her head into his shoulder. He flew to the top of the wall which divided the garden from farmland, and called to her again.

In this way did Barbara return by stages, guided by her mate, a bird young enough to be her great-great-grandson, first to the guttering of the roof, then painfully up the slates to the window of the loft. The labour was great, and perhaps pointless, since she could easily have been caught at ground level and carried upstairs, but seemed to the tenants heroic in both birds. When she was inside, one tenant went up to the loft to examine her. The other consulted books.

The diseases of pigeons are mysterious. There are nostrums and pills to be bought in pet shops to cure ills which are not even listed in the literature, and the literature itself is contradictory. What is pigeon pox to one author may be a one-eye cold to another; canker, roup and coryza are held by one to be different names for the same condition, by another to require three different forms of treatment. Some authors suggest that pigeons who fall sick should be killed; they are not worth curing; they will never amount to anything. Others advocate treatment as expensive and picturesque as daily injections of penicillin into the chest muscle. The tenants were repelled by the first and dismayed by the second. They were further confused by the circumstance that Almighty God, in His infinite providence, has provided pigeons with more diseases than symptoms, so that, whether beset by virus, bacterium or internal parasite, the bird behaves in very much the same way.

Like the physicians of ancient Alexandria, pigeon-doctors carefully scrutinize the droppings of their patients. Barbara's droppings were scrutinized. They told the tenants that she was sick. Her mouth and throat were examined. No cheesy growths, therefore not canker. (The tenants had never seen a cheesy growth, but assumed that they would know one if they saw it.) She was not sneezing. Her ceres were not discoloured. This, although a negative observation, was in fact most helpful, for a discolouration of the ceres is a symptom for so many diseases that her not having it narrowed the field considerably.

'Do you think she could be egg-bound?'

'She doesn't lay eggs.'

'Having lost the habit could make it more likely. "Failure to pass an egg may be due to an excess of fat." Put it this way: is she squatting on the floor of the coop with her tail elevated?'

It was not a position which Barbara would ever allow herself to adopt, nor had she done so. Even in distress, even in a cardboard box among Petlita, she remained a lady of the old school.

'Is her vent inflamed?'

Barbara's vent was examined. Perhaps it was a little inflamed.

'Is there further evidence of swelling?'

In so plump a bird, evidence of swelling was not easy to detect, but yes; perhaps there was such evidence. Yes, there was an area which seemed distended and tight to the touch, and when it was touched seemed to cause Barbara discomfort – which is the word used among medical persons instead of 'pain'.

There was the sound of a beak tapping against the landing window. The Fantail had taken up station outside.

The treatment for egg-binding begins with castor oil, and it is another of the deficiencies of the literature that the words 'a good dose' are used where some more exact definition of quantity would have been more helpful to worried tenants doing their inexperienced best. It did no good. There is a suggestion that the egg should be punctured by a knitting needle, and the bits of shell picked out with tweezers. The tenants did not feel able to undertake such an operation. Instead they followed another course, which was to annoint Barbara's vent with olive oil (against scalding) and hold it – and consequently her – over steam, while gently massaging the area behind the egg. Barbara endured it all. It did no good.

Treatment continued over two days, while the Fantail waited and called, and Barbara grew weaker. She did not struggle; she did not even complain; she took food and water as it was offered, and she endured the treatment. At the end, humiliated but undefeated, she turned her face to the wall and died in the night.

It was the first disaster of a disastrous summer. Pigeons had died before at the teeth of the stoat, and two had disappeared for a reason which only later became clear. Nestlings had been neglected and trampled by their own parents, and their tiny naked bodies thrown like mice over a dividing wall. But a broken leg had been mended, a damaged wing restored by rest, external parasites eradicated. Where there had been sickness, it had been of little account: rest, isolation and the addition of vitamins to the drinking water had cured it – or had appeared to do so. Now there was sickness, and it was of great account, and nothing cured it.

It began with a Chinese Owl. She was a Cream, intended as a mate for Ginge, intended that they should produce together a line of delicious Creams, but the eggs were infertile and the birds had to be separated, she to live among the hens, he to mate (again unsuccessfully) with a White. She established herself on a perch, kept company for a while with another hen until the tenants should get around to pairing her again, and did nothing particularly remarkable in the meantime until one day she began to jerk her head.

The loft was divided into three sections. Cocks and hens considered suitable for breeding but not actually, as one might say, 'at it', were separated from each other and from the Main Loft by wire netting, each sex provided with a sufficiency of perches and its own complement of food, water, grit and minerals. In the Main Loft were birds of no particular pedigree kept for sentimental reasons and as foster parents, some young birds, and some birds securely paired, who might be hatching their own eggs or raising their own squeakers and who were given preference in the allotment of the nestboxes which had been provided in three tiers along one wall. Most of the nestboxes were occupied, then, by breeding pairs or by foster parents who held them by right of custom and practice and could well defend them, but a few were the object of constant dispute, so that Wilf and Wendell, like many gay couples elsewhere, sometimes enjoyed the comfort and privacy of a home of their own, and were sometimes ousted by intolerant heterosexuals desperate for a place to nest. The Main Loft had access to the window, and the Main Loft birds, Squeak among them, went freely in and out.

Any oddity of behaviour, therefore, was more likely to be noticed early in one of the Main Loft birds, so that the tenants could not know when the Cream Chinese Owl had begun to jerk her head. It was certainly causing restlessness among the other hens, who, insofar as the confines of their area allowed them to do so, had put space between her and themselves; even her some-time companion had deserted her.

She cowered in a corner. The tenant, whose purpose in entering the loft had been merely to remove unwanted eggs and to contemplate for a while the life of the community, picked her up carefully. There was a moment's panic, followed by unnatural submission. She seemed light, but it is as easy to imagine lightness in pigeons as it is in humankind to imagine an itch. She twisted her head sideways. Was something lodged in her throat? Nothing. Was there a difficulty in breathing? It was hard to tell. Once again a cardboard box was set on the landing, and there was a recourse to pigeon literature.

Keep Your Pigeons Flying by Leon F. Whitney, DVM,* a member of the Pathology Department at the School of Medicine at Yale, was the book most often consulted by the tenants. It has a Diagnostic Table of Symptoms, beginning with Anaemia (which may be due to fleas), on through Abnormal Moulting and Thirst, by way of Blindness and Convulsions, right down to Wattles, Discoloration of, and Wheezing (observed in Newcastle Disease, as anyone who has ever been to Newcastle will readily confirm). Was the Cream Chinese Owl offering evidence of Breathing, Abnormal (Air-sac mites, Aspergillosis, Malaria), the tenants wondered, or Nervous Movements (Paratyphoid, Puffinosis, Poisoning)?

Of the twelve ailments with which abnormal breath-

*Faber and Faber, London, 1968.

ing is commonly associated, infectious coryza seemed to be the most likely. The presenting symptoms are sneezing, coughing, clearing the throat, together with a nasal discharge and swollen eyes, the same as those of a human cold, in fact, except that in pigeons the ceres become discoloured also. Was the Cream sneezing? She certainly seemed to have something wrong with her throat. But was this twisting action not more a Nervous Movement and therefore indicating the condition described by Dr Whitney when the bacterium of paratyphoid invades the brain? 'The pigeon may twist its head always to one side' (yes, exactly that), 'put its head between its legs or pull its head backwards until it falls' (the pigeon, the tenants assumed, not the head: anyway the Cream was doing neither). Dr Whitney's book, although it was by far the most comprehensive of those owned by the tenants, was not the most clear. It seemed to suggest that this manifestation of inflammation of the brain was confined to young birds – squabs and squeakers – and that older birds suffering from paratyphoid developed swellings beneath the wings or on the legs, that their joints stiffened and they had difficulty in flying. The Cream was three years old and had no swellings.

None of the other books mentioned inflammation of the brain in paratyphoid at all, though they were all strong on tumours and stiff joints. How was the Cream to be treated? Infectious coryza is treated with antibiotics, paratyphoid by lancing the tumours. The tenants had no antibiotics and the bird no tumours. There seemed nothing for it, but to keep her, with food and water, in isolation lest she should infect the others. At least she was in no immediate danger; the literature was clear on that. Though paratyphoid is a killer of young birds, adults invariably recover, while infectious coryza 'drags on for weeks': there would be time to get antibiotics from the vet. They loosely closed the top of the box, and left her with soothing words. She died, as Barbara had done, in the night, probably at that thin time between dark and dawn, when life slips so easily away from the sick and the distressed.

The tenants were away in London for two days that week. When they returned they found what seemed at first to be a dusty bundle of feathers on the floor in a corner of the loft. It was Speck One, mother of Speck Two, crested, affectionate, intelligent, most loved. She had been one of the six originals, bought from a baker in Birmingham, kept (as has to be) for six weeks behind wire netting so that she should forget the bakery, and then released. The tenants, who had bought her ignorantly for her looks, had not known she was a high flier and, when she had disappeared on release high in the air beyond their sight, they believed her flown away, and had gone gloomily back indoors. And then an hour later, first a speck, a mote of dust high in the blue, then gradually descending, this bird. She had landed, taken corn from a hand, remained thereafter in her new home, always delighting in flight though never again so high, because she could find none to fly so high with her. They had called her Speck because she had, that first time, dwindled to a speck, and also because she was speckled all over with grey. She had mated with a white dove, had been dissuaded from nesting in the woodshed, had produced issue, notably Speck Two and a deplorable black bird with a white collar known as the Reverend. None of her issue had been crested, none had flown high, none had inherited her gentle nature. She had been unique.

Now she was dust again, huddled and dead in a corner, ignored by the other birds. The tenants would not be sentimental. No burial, no nonsense of that sort. One of the tenants took the corpse to the edge of the wood, and left it there. Let the crows and magpies have her, let the foxes have her, let the carrion-eaters have her; she was mere carrion now, as we all shall be. That evening, the same unsentimental tenant left the dinner table in tears.

And in the morning, the Fantail was sick.

There was fear in the loft. Squeak felt it. Her perch at night was the top of an interior door, so that she roosted above the purpose-built perches of the segregated cocks and hens and most of the perches and nestboxes of the Main Loft. She heard birds shifting restlessly below her, and felt their fear rise up from below like an exhalation in the darkness. When morning came she would fly to the window and remain there, looking out for the tenants. She had seen the Cream go into a convulsion, fluttering its wings crazily, and reaching up into the air as if to pluck flies, and the panic flight of the other hens away from it and against the wire. She had seen Speck leave her nestbox at evening, and shuffle into a corner to die. She had heard the Fantail moaning in the night and in the morning struggle to reach water, ignored and avoided by the other birds. These birds were not of her kind, but she lived among them; they were her companions, and she felt their fear.

The tenants took the Fantail from the loft to some other place. Squeak moved from the window to the coping of the roof, thence to the top of the bird table, waiting for one or both of the tenants to leave the house. It was a day of cloud and light wind, perhaps with rain to come, not the weather for an outdoor lunch, or an afternoon spent in garden chairs, reading, scribbling or simply taking the sun. The tenants would, however, at some time emerge.

One came out with plastic shopping-bags, and carrying a box, but went immediately to the car, so that Squeak, who had taken off in flight to board him, turned back to a windowsill. (The Fantail was in that box, on his way to the vet in Shipston.) Later the other tenant emerged, to gaze anxiously at the sky, where Speck Two was leading a group of agitated birds which included his widowed father, the white dove, in aimless wheeling flight around the house.

She must grasp her time when it came: to wait for a convenient moment was not in her nature. She flew down to the tenant, refusing thereafter to be dislodged, so that she must willy-nilly be carried indoors. Squeak had no attachments to her companions in the loft. At a time of fear, families draw together; Squeak's place was with these parents who continued to provide food and security. She refused to leave the tenants all that day and, when attempts were made to return her to the loft, resisted them. That night, though the supply of cardboard boxes which had once contained wine was already somewhat depleted, she slept in the tenants' room.

Antibiotics were obtained from the vet, and given to the Fantail, which died, and its corpse was taken to the wood. Vitamins, to build resistance, and the cure-all preparation from Holland were added to the drinking water. It did no good. Three Chinese Owls of no particular individuality died, the Reverend died, and went to the wood. A Carpet Slipper died, and three squeakers. Magpie, a pied black-and-white pseudo-Fantail whose mother had mated beneath her, died, and Magpie's mother died. The tenants consulted members of the Fancy, who spoke gloomily and at length of epidemics which had wiped out the entire populations of certain lofts. These lofts, the members of the Fancy hinted, had not been well maintained.

At last there came a time when no more birds sickened. The symptoms of all the sick had been various. None, after the Cream, had exhibited the disorientation of an inflamed brain. There had been fluffed-out feathers, loss of appetite, discoloured wattles and ceres, green and liquid droppings, apparent difficulties in breathing, most of the symptoms listed in Dr Whitney's helpful Diagnostic Table, either singly or in combination. Two, like Speck, had died before the tenants had been able to observe any symptoms at all, and as for the squeakers, they were young, and might have died from neglect. The epidemic, like some Biblical plague, had erupted without warning, and ceased as suddenly.

The plagues of the Bible are known to have a cause: you have annoyed some prophet, or refused emigration visas to Israelites. The tenants never discovered what killed their pigeons, whether it was the *Eimeria columbae*, the internal parasite which causes coccidiosis, the *Salmonella typhi-murium* of paratyphoid, the *Hemiphilus gallinarum* of infectious coryza, or simply, as they later preferred to believe, a consignment of old and mouldy peanuts which may have nurtured the fungus of aspergillosis. It is easier, after all, and perhaps more prudent, to blame a peanut than the Lord of Hosts.

The hand-rearing of small birds can become addictive. Human children seem hardly to grow at all; they seem always to have been the size they are, and only old snapshots and pencil lines drawn on the kitchen wall prove otherwise. But birds reach adulthood with astonishing speed, though they do not thereafter seem to change very much; selfishness and loneliness, failure and despair, self-indulgence and pain and fear of death do not mark the features of pigeons as they do of humankind. Squeak had been hand-reared by accident, but she was well and strong and had resisted the epidemic. Moreover, she seemed to have no fear of humans, even of strangers, whereas birds born and reared in the loft were, for the most part, a nervy lot, and given to panic if approached too suddenly. Why should not these admirable, accidentally achieved qualities of Squeak be fostered in other young birds, and by design? The tenants resolved to set about it.

They would not start with birds as young as Squeak had been; there would be danger in that. Nestlings three weeks old, already taking semi-solid food, should do well enough. They would be hand-fed at first, then learn to pick for themselves. They would commute, when necessary, in boxes between Warwickshire and South Kensington. They would be as affectionate as puppies, and as tame.

The plague had interrupted the breeding programme. Now that it was over, the pigeons were set to breed in earnest. A cock and hen who, even though separated by chicken wire, had clung to it daily, one on each side like Pyramus and Thisbe, he calling 'Do not forget me,' she attempting to bill him through the wire, even these constant lovers were ruthlessly assigned new partners, and came in time to accept them. Ginge, who had failed to produce issue with the Cream, failed again with the White, and was now put to a plump Mealie. He accepted the change cheerfully. Femininity was all one to him. He had the sailor's easy ways – 'If it moves, mate with it.' Even Wendell and Wilf gave Ginge a wary eye. This time his eggs were fertile. He became *paterfamilias* but sired no champions.

The tenants, truth to tell, were not good at breeding their birds. Their aspirations were high but their hearts were soft. However skilful a pairing, the chances are that at least one, and probably both, of the two nestlings produced at a laying will be mismarked or in some way unsatisfactory, and one cannot tell if this is so until they are two weeks old. At this point, unsatisfactory squeakers should be 'culled', which is the word used to disguise the actual process of wringing their necks. 'When you are dealing with livestock, you must not have any qualms about terminating substandard life. If culled in the early stages, future trouble and unnecessary feeding of retarded squeakers will be avoided' – it is the assured asyntactical voice of established authority: not, as one might have guessed, from a speech of Adolf Hitler, but from the Pet Library's *Pigeon Guide* by Claude R. Hill.* And indeed pigeon squeakers do as the inmates of the concentration camps were said to do; they make it easy for you to cull them by looking so unattractive, whereas it requires the callousness of a Cruft's Exhibitor to drown mismarked puppies. Nevertheless, the tenants had found they could

*Racing Pigeon, London, 1980.

not do it, and their breeding programme was much restricted in consequence.

However, points are given at shows for 'well presented' birds; that is, birds which do not cower at the back of a pen, but will inspect a judge's fingers with dignified interest, and allow themselves to be held in intimate ways without protest. Hand-rearing would look after that; the tenants would acquire a name for well-presented birds. Six nestlings, Owls of pedigree, were chosen. They were separated from parents or foster parents. In both Warwickshire and South Kensington, architectural fantasies of cardboard and green garden netting were created for them over sheets of newspaper Sellotaped together. They were fed in the way the tenants preferred, which was the opening of mouths by fingers, and the shovelling in of nourishing grains and pellets. They disliked the process as much as Squeak had done, and quickly learned to feed themselves, rushing all together with an agitated waggling of wings to peck first from a hand, then from a dish, six small birds squeaking in concert as they ate, like choirboys gobbling Smarties during the anthem.

Being kept apart, they did not impinge on Squeak's way of life. After the passing of the plague she had been returned to the loft, and had ceased to commute. She kept her post at the window, watched for the tenants and flew down to them whenever they emerged from house or car, was with them while they were out of doors, and waited for them while they were within. She ignored the other pigeons, except when they intruded on her space, and did not demand access to the tenants' space, provided that she received respect and reassurance from them in the space which was common to all.

The six squeakers were not brought into that space, not at this time, and Squeak had no second sight to divine the contents of cardboard boxes.

The squeakers grew, acquired plumage, became individuals, and were given names – Smudge, who was the colour of wood ash; Spot, a dun hen, said to have a white spot at the base of her tail, which only one tenant could see; Dickie, a blue chequer with a dickie bow; Sam and Sally (for no better reason than that, being Saddles, their names might as well begin with S), and Mungo who, having an exploring nature, was named for Mungo Park.

In time they were brought out, as Squeak had been, to enjoy the sun on the patio. There were six of them; they were used to each others' company, and knew that they were pigeons. They did not cower in corners but established space for themselves on top of the low wall which divided the patio from the drive and next to which the tenants habitually sat. From this they were able, as they grew daring and dextrous, to jump on to a lap or knee, whence they might make the ascent up stomach and chest to a shoulder, or, more hazardously, descend to the ground by way of a leg.

Squeak was puzzled. These creatures seemed to be intimate with her parents. Were they of the same kind? They walked over ground which was hers, and were not prevented. She perched on a head, and inspected them. They paid her no attention. She hopped down on to a shoulder. They retreated before her, squeaking. She remained. One, after some while, began the ascent towards her. She moved her head forwards, and it rolled down back among the lower slopes. Well, whatever it was, it did not threaten her. She pecked lightly at the ear next to her, to indicate that, if hemp were offered, it would not be refused.

The tenant gave hemp instead to the small object and to two other objects which came to join it.

The shock was so very great that Squeak did not know which most to blame, that which gave or those who took. Should she descend at once to the massacre of the intruders below, or first draw blood from the traitor's ear? She discovered that she lacked the will to do either, but remained where she was in shock.

One of the tenants said to the other, 'Just as well Squeak's not jealous.'

It was only noise to Squeak, but the tenor of the noise was clear. There was approval for what was happening; there was concern for these objects. Three more of them were on the top of the wall close to her. She left the tenant's shoulder, and attacked them savagely.

And was knocked off the wall by the hand of a tenant, striking at her.

She returned to the top of the bird table. She knew, in that part of a bird or animal which does know what is natural and what is not, that it was natural that her parents should in time reject her. But some part of this had already happened. She had a place of her own, lived apart from them, yet continued to receive titbits and attention from them. They had never nested again. Until they did, or until she herself, she, Squeak, found a mate and nested, there was no occasion for rejection on either side. Until now. Had they nested, unknown to her? Were these small objects the further young of her own kind? And she? With whom was she to nest, now that she had been displaced from theirs?

She looked across at the tenants, and sorrowed at

what must be. She had no choice; of all her kind, there were only these two, and herself, and now perhaps the small objects who were beneath her notice. If she was to find a mate, it must be from one of these. She looked across at the tenants, and knew she was in love.

FOUR

In Love

THE TENANTS still believed that Squeak was male.
They had little evidence for this, but larger beliefs are
held on less. She was territorial; she could be aggressive;
she displayed no particularly female characteristics;
anyway, they had always called her 'he'. They assumed
that in time Squeak would choose and court some
mismarked or underfeathered hen of the Main Loft, and
settle into a pairing. They would have their own nestbox:
Squeak was owed so much. The hen would lay. The eggs
could not be kept, of course; the tenants wanted no more
cockney pigeons to scoff expensive grains bought for

their betters, but perhaps Squeak and his mate would enjoy the emotional fulfilment of rearing a family vicariously by being permitted to foster. If not, it was of no importance. Pigeons are dedicated parents, but the dedication is soon transferred; the true attachment of a pigeon is to its mate.

Squeak herself did not at first know what to do. *She never told her love, but let concealment like a worm i' the bud* . . . it is the business of a hen to wait. It is usual for pigeons to lay two eggs at a time, usual for the hatched birds to be one male, one female; there is no great disparity of numbers among cocks and hens in a dovecote or in the wild, and pigeons seldom experience the sexual deprivations of well brought up young ladies after a World War. Squeak had only to *be*. Sooner or later – and probably sooner – a cock would display himself before her, not by waiting in a dark corner and opening his macintosh, but by strutting, puffing out his neck, dragging his tail on the ground, eventually calling her to a nest already chosen, perhaps attempting to drive her to it, and she would go with him if she wished, and if not, avoid him. Several cocks of the Main Loft had, in fact, already behaved in just such a manner to her, but since they were not of her own kind she had not known what they were about, and had struck out angrily and flapped her wings at those who had crowded her, thus confirming the tenants in their belief that she herself was a cock.

The tenants, however, though they were of Squeak's own kind, showed no signs of wanting to drive her to a nest, even when she sometimes walked in front of them in the manner of one willing to be driven. Blind, blind fools! What was so close to them, they could not see. She brooded. They worried whether she might be sickening for something, and dosed her with vitamins. She seriously considered the possibility that they might not know what they had to do, and demonstrated by dragging her own tail before them on the composition-stone flags of the patio. Knowing her to be male, they looked about for the hen to whom she must be displaying.

Meanwhile the matter of the small objects which had invaded her territory solved itself. The objects grew and became merely birds of the same sort as those with whom she already shared the loft; indeed, they were soon put among the others to share it with her. They did not cease because of that to invade her territory, the heads, shoulders and laps of the tenants, and were still fed when they did so, but they gave way as soon as Squeak herself appeared to reclaim it, and, if they did not, she chased them off. The tenants gave no indication that any of the six had been chosen as mates, nor did they break with Squeak. Certain small intimacies took place, the nibbling of an ear or the tiny feathers on the backs of their necks on Squeak's part, a gentle scratching of her own neck or breast with the longest of a set of five beaks on theirs, but these intimacies did not lead to mating. The tenants did not display. They would not drive her. *They had not chosen a nest.*

The cocks of the Main Loft knew perfectly well that Squeak was a hen, and although devoted in the way of egg-hatching and chick-rearing to their own partners, were not above attempting to cover her on a casual basis. She took no more notice of these attempts than of the more proper attempts to court her, and should one, by whatever sudden pounce or momentary distraction of her attention, succeed in mounting her, would move away,

71

leaving him floundering. The morals of pigeons in this respect are suburban. There will always be time for extra-marital affairs after a pairing, but first things first.

It was high summer, and one of those rare English summers in which the sun shines unbrokenly, day after day. Tar softened on the roads, and bare feet burned on the patio. Warnings of drought were given, beginning as always in the south-west, but working up to the Midlands. In Herefordshire and Worcestershire, Gloucestershire and Oxfordshire, up into Warwickshire, the grass grew yellow and the rivers low. The tenants had a garden pool of their own in which trout, bought from a hatchery, had once lived (a heron ate them), and it was fed by its own spring, so that they were in that respect independent of the Severn–Trent Water Authority, and might water their flowers and vegetables by bucket, which nightly they did, watched by Squeak. All that they did in the open air was watched by Squeak, and they were much in the open air.

She had been reared in a flat, was quartered now in the attic; she knew that the open air was not for nesting. Why did they remain so long outdoors? They did not fly, took no baths, and when they ate brought the food out with them. Sometimes they lay on the lawn by the pool, next to the weeping pear. Was that their choice? Squeak lay between them, watching one with each eye. The texture of the grass was not unpleasant, though hardly up to carpet, and it lacked the security of a cardboard box. Though she was not yet a year old, she had been born with the knowledge that a nest should be above ground, hidden from sight from above, that access to it should be restricted; it should be private. None of this could be said of the lawn by the pool.

It must be indoors. They showed no interest in the nestboxes of the Main Loft, and indeed there would hardly be room for them there, and no need since they had the run of the house, just as she herself had, being of their kind. The nest would be inside the house but away from where the birds lived. If the tenants would not call her to it, she must find it for herself.

It was true that the inside of the house was still Squeak's territory, but she no longer visited it often. Like some Ottoman emperor, she knew that it was there, and it was hers, and that was enough. Sometimes the tenants, in an attempt to reduce the débris of feathers and droppings which accumulated in the loft, would shoo most of the birds outside for the day, and close the attic window. On such a day Squeak might take a whim to return indoors and, being the only pigeon who knew that there was a way to the loft inside the house, and the only pigeon who would, except in dire emergency, be allowed to take it, would communicate her whim to any tenant within her reach by first flying to the tenant, then immediately afterwards to the front door at which she would stare fixedly, after which she would look back at the tenant, then to the door again, until that door would be opened, and Squeak would mount two flights of stairs, and wait outside the door to the loft until that was opened also. It was one of the frustrations of her present position that a mere whim should be easily communicated to the tenants, whereas the desire which dominated her almost to the exclusion of all others could not be communicated at all.

All around her the birds of the loft were breeding. The plague deaths had been forgotten. Life quickened in the loft. Hideously complacent birds spread themselves over eggs, some of which had been laid not even in a nestbox but anyhow in corners on the floor. The tenants would, after a while, take these eggs away, sometimes even tread on one by accident, but the miasma of mother-hood remained. The air was full of the sound of squeaking. She watched the nestlings fall over each other in the hustle for food, watched the parent birds pumping it into them, and she hated and despised them all.

When next she indicated to a tenant that she wished to be allowed indoors, she did not at once mount the stairs. Instead she accompanied the tenant to the kitchen, and watched while salads and salami were put on plates. The tenant moved rapidly about, did not settle on any suitable surface, and did not call her: the nest would not be here. She repaired to the living-room, shat briefly on *Harbinger Bird IV* for old times' sake, and inspected the sofa closely. It was not entirely suitable, being too exposed in the centre, but it would do. She waited on it. The tenant came and went, bearing plates, wholemeal bread and iced cider to the patio. So much for the sofa. Squeak mounted to the first floor. She inspected two bedrooms and a bathroom. There were many prospective nests, desirable residences with vacant possession, and she tried them all, but if the tenants had chosen one, they said nothing of that to her.

'Where's Squeak?'

'Upstairs, I think.'

'Does he want in?'

'No, I don't think so. He's exploring bedrooms.'

'Extraordinary bird!'

Very well, she herself must choose a nest. It was not proper, but she would do it.

She returned to the kitchen. The tenants appeared to spend more of their time in that room than in any other. (Squeak did not count bedrooms, since time spent asleep is not time at all, nor, except during the plague, had she herself spent time with them during the night.) The kitchen was not a place of soft surfaces, though something could always be improvised with twigs and pieces of straw. She flew up on to the kitchen table, and looked about her. The windowsill would not do. Through the window she could see the tenants eating lunch, and beyond them the valley. The window was open to predators of all sorts from field and barn, and although she had some small experience that the air in the windowframe was of a special sort and had in the past proved impenetrable, she could not be sure that it would always be so – water, after all, was sometimes solid and sometimes liquid, and the air itself changed from day to day in other ways, sometimes throwing one about, sometimes translucent instead of transparent, sometimes wet; no, air was chancy stuff, and the windowsill would not do. There was another smaller window in another wall, and the door would be a poor barrier against predators since it was often opened. As far into the room as possible and backed by a wall with no windows would be best, but with some form of protection on one's flank.

In the back wall (no door, no window) was a solid projection, like a buttress at one side, running from floor to ceiling (it was a double oven, with cupboards above and below). Next to it was another projection from the wall, raised well above the ground (the refrigerator, with a tray on top of it, and a work surface to one side). On top of the projection was . . . she flew over to inspect it: yes, it was of soft material (an oven glove); it would make a nest.

She crouched on the oven glove, and began to call.

The window and the door were both open. The tenants heard her.

'Is that Squeaky? I thought you said he was upstairs.'

'He was.'

Perhaps some other bird had found its way, unnoticed, into the kitchen, and had chosen a nest, just as once Speck One had attempted to nest in the woodshed. If so, that bird must be discouraged. The kitchen was not for pigeons; food was left uncovered there. Each of the tenants waited for the other to make a move, and at last one did so. And discovered Squeak crouched on the oven glove.

'What do you think *you're* doing?'

She had called, and a tenant had come. She was not foolish; she knew she could not mate with both. This one would do. She called the tenant urgently to the glove. Once they had established a home, the act of mating could be performed anywhere.

'Extraordinary bird!' The tenant picked her up, and carried her outside. 'Sitting on an oven glove, calling his heart out.'

'Calling? He hasn't mated, has he? I certainly haven't seen him chasing anyone around. Extraordinary bird!'

Squeak was released. She sat for a while on the tenant's knee, and then returned to the kitchen. She did not fly there, but walked, looking back twice before turning the corner inside the front door.

'An oven glove?'

'*The* oven glove. We only have the one.' Squeak could be heard calling again. The other tenant went in to the kitchen. Squeak faced the tenant, sat well forward, lifted her tail, nodded her head, summoned the tenant to join her on the nest. The tenant went back outside.

'He's nodding his head.'

'Well, you know they do.'

'When they're courting. Who's he courting? There's no one in the kitchen.'

A pause. 'Well, not quite no one, I suppose,' the other tenant said.

'Oh God!' The tenant went briskly back into the kitchen, picked Squeak off the oven glove, and hung it on a hook. Squeak made the 'How dare you!' noise which is so close to the 'Oh God! Trouble!' noise that one has to know a bird and its circumstances before the two can be distinguished – and was carried back to the patio, and the front door shut. There she was given hemp. 'I suppose I should be flattered.'

'Extraor –'

'Oh, shut up saying that.' The tenant brooded. 'Imprinted!'

'He's very bright; he'll get over it. The sheer impracticality of it will get to him. There are hens all around; he'll make the adjustment.'

Squeak gave herself to thought. Clearly the tenants were in some respects retarded. Neither was likely to make a mate of quality: she would mate with neither if she had a choice but, such as they were, they were the choice she had. Other creatures of their kind and hers came to the house from time to time, but one must assume that they were mated already, since they did not stay, and took little notice of Squeak: one, who had very long feathers on the top of its head into which Squeak had anchored her claws, had become upset, and had behaved towards Squeak much as Squeak herself be-haved towards those cock birds which had attempted to tread her on the patio. The tenants did take notice of

Squeak: both did. They were generous with endearments as with food, would bill as best they could, tickle the side of her neck, make free with the feathers of her chest, gently scratch at her beak with one of theirs. Only they never seemed to want to go further.

It was of no use to call them from the patio to a nest in the kitchen; they did not come. She must stay always with them, and when they returned to the kitchen, indicate the attractions of the oven glove.

The tenants remained for much of the day outdoors, and so did Squeak. Whenever they ventured in, she ventured with them. When, that evening as every evening, the piece of plastic trellis over the attic window was removed so that the pigeons might return to their nestboxes and perches, Squeak did not return, but remained with the tenants. Light cooking, suitable for a summer evening, was to be done. The oven glove was needed, and taken from its hook. Squeak at once sat on it, and began to call. She was picked off the glove, and carried upstairs to the loft, and so ended the first day of her courting.

The second day was much like the first. Squeak remained with the tenants, wherever they happened to be. When they separated, she chose, if she were allowed, the one indoors, but was not often allowed. She did not call to them except in the kitchen. The oven glove was moved about, but as long as it was horizontal, she sat on it.

On the third day she tried a new tactic. Hitherto she had believed that nesting should come first, and coupling follow. That was the rational way: first furnish the home, and give birth thereafter. However, it had begun to appear that the tenants held the contrary conviction, and would not make jam where they had not tasted the fruit. *Oh, soldier, soldier, will you marry me?* – so many virgins, both wise and foolish, had shared Squeak's predicament, been pushed to the same hard choice. Give all, and lose all; give nowt, and gain nowt. But she was a pigeon; she did not agonize over risks; she had chosen already, and must abide by that choice. Let them have their will of her. If eggs should be the result, the tenants would have to take their turns in sitting, and what price then the oven glove?

She sat upon the bare knee of a tenant and watched a chaffinch trying to pick maize from a crack between flagstones. The tenant lazily caressed her neck. She crouched, head down, tail spread; she was ready. 'Oh God!' the tenant said, 'Are we sure Squeak's a cock?'

But they had seen Wilf and Wendell exchange roles often enough; one never knew what a pigeon would choose to do in sexual matters. The other tenant said, 'He's confused, I expect. I mean, since you won't mate with him, he's trying to tell you what to do. Or else it's a submission ritual.'

'A what?'

'You know; it was on television. Apes do it. The younger apes bare their behinds to older ones as a symbolic submission. They do it in Sumatra – Gibraltar – West Africa somewhere: it was on one of those nature programmes. All it really means is, "Don't hit me." '

'I wasn't going to hit him. I was just stroking his neck.'

Squeak remained where she was. The sun glinted on the short feathers of her throat and the back of her neck, iridescent, green and purple and bronze. The white bar at the base of her tail was a notice, saying 'Come on.' She was glossy and healthy and ready for love, and she was offering herself to tenants who had not even, except in the most desultory way, courted her. Pride, independence of spirit, the proper and natural order of behaviour, all had been discarded; her submission was complete. The tenant tickled her neck again, and placed a hand under her head. She sank her head completely into the hand, and buried her beak between the fingers, uttering small sounds of content and encouragement. The other tenant said, 'I shouldn't do that if I were you. It seems to set him off.'

She offered herself many times that day and the next to the unresponsive tenants. They believed (as was the case) that she had become imprinted on themselves. Since the Other One had died so early, she had been reared as a single nestling, unlike the other hand-reared birds, who had grown up amid green garden netting in a clutch of six, knowing themselves to be pigeons. It had not occurred to the tenants before that they were Squeak's parents, but they realized it now, and were ready to make allowances for odd behaviour to which they felt that they themselves had contributed. However, they continued to believe (as was not the case) that Squeak was a cock bird, making confused signals of sexual submission in an attempt to find a mate.

It seemed to them that they had better find a mate for Squeak themselves, and they therefore confined her with another hen in one of those compartmented cases in which birds are carried to shows. At first the partition between the two birds was kept in place to allow them to become used to each other before a more close acquaintance. Squeak did not know why she was being punished by being shut in a box. There was another creature in the box with her. Perhaps it was being punished also, but that was of no importance; its irrelevant presence did not ease the pain she felt at being deprived of the company of tenants. She called sadly, persistently, to them. Her calling could be heard all over the house and on the patio. The tenants came, after some time, and removed the partition. Squeak immediately attacked the other hen most viciously with beak and wings, since it was clearly an alien being, intruding upon her grief and on her territory, and perhaps having designs of its own upon the tenants. The hen had no stomach for a fight, and tried to escape. A cardboard box would have split. The carrying-case, being of aluminium, merely rocked on the uneven floor of elm planks, and dust rose around it. The tenants opened the lid of the box, and attempted to remove the frightened hen, which escaped through unsteady hands and perched on a rafter, not to be retrieved until the evening. Squeak flew up to a shoulder, and remained there, turning on the spot and making noises of indignant outrage which the tenants took only as further proof of maleness.

It could not be allowed to continue. Squeak must be confined. Alone in a box would be too cruel. There remained the two pens in which cocks and hens were separately kept before being paired for breeding. The tenants did not propose to confine Squeak with the hens, some of whom he might impregnate with his cockney genes, yet with other cocks he might fight, being lovesick and quick to anger. There was debate, which grew acerbic, between the tenants, and in the end Squeak was confined with the cocks.

Shut up, away from the tenants, away from the window, away even from her usual perch in the Main Loft, she moped, drooped, was not seen to eat, refused hemp when it was offered, and turned her face to the wall. A pigeon faces the wall when it is going to die. Alarmed, the tenants returned Squeak to the Main Loft. She went at once to the window, remained on station there until she saw a tenant come out on to the patio, and flew down to be reunited with her own true love.

The tenants thought again. This phase would pass. You are burdened with a delinquent infant, seeking attention, or a senile parent who cannot in decency be consigned to a mental hospital, (and anyway the National Health Service has no beds): 'Ignore him,' you say. It is the way. The infant will in time, not getting the attention he has been seeking, give over his aggressive behaviour and respond to reason. The senile parent will, in time and by God's grace, die. All passes. The tenants would be kind but firm, considerate but unresponsive to Squeak's demands. For his own good – only for that – he would be for the time being excluded from the interior of the house, cut off from the oven glove, denied the little physical intimacies which might so easily awaken lust, but allowed in other respects his usual freedom, and in time his passion would turn another way.

And they would continue to try to interest him in hens. Like those who, in an attempt to distract James I from his infatuation with the Duke of Buckingham, took the young man Manson, washed his face with posset curd and set him in the King's way, the tenants would trail before Squeak the most enticing hens, even show birds, who could always be taken away again once they had achieved the transference. All passes; this too would pass.

They allowed Squeak access to them on the patio, then went indoors for lunch. The kitchen window was open. They could be clearly seen at the table, and beyond them, no doubt, would lie the oven glove. Squeak knew, as has been said, that the air in the kitchen window was dodgy stuff, more likely than not to turn solid on a person, but a person must do what a person has to do. She set herself on course for the window, and luckily the air was not against her, and let her through. She landed on the table, inspected a quiche briefly, decided that it held no interest for her, found the oven glove on a further work surface, settled on it, and called.

Sweet reason ruled. A tenant picked Squeak up gently, and carried her outside; the other tenant shut the window. Squeak set herself on the same course again, and this time the air had turned solid. She landed heavily against it, beak first, and fell to the ground. A tenant said, 'Jesus!'

'I'll go and get him.'

'No, he's all right.'

Squeak was more surprised than hurt at the solidity of the air, which had, after all, allowed her free passage only a moment before. She shook her head to clear away any residual dizziness, tested her wings, and found them to be in good order. She flew up to the windowsill, and tapped the air in the window experimentally. (The tenants thought that she was knocking for entry, and determined to ignore it.) Well, the air was certainly solid now. It would need some effort to get through. She took station on top of the bird table, and tried again. The air resisted her; she thought her beak would be forced back into her head. She tried again, this time turning upwards at the last moment so as to break through with her feet, and fell back into a flower bed.

'He'll do himself a damage.'

'We can't give in.'

'Finish your salad, and we'll get back outside. I can't stand much more of this.'

'He's got to learn.'

Squeak discovered that she was a little dizzy. It would be better to take time, and to consider for a while the nature of this solid air if she were to find a way either of forcing through it or inducing it to revert to a natural state. This was her own problem. She did not blame the tenants for ignoring her manifest distress; she did not require their aid. It is not the business of the courted to make matters easy for their suitors, and since to be a suitor was the task which, against the natural order, had fallen to her and which she had accepted, she must succeed in mating by her own efforts. She rested on the windowsill, and fixed her gaze on the tenants within. One stared back at her; the other shifted uncomfortably, and looked away.

The day had been overcast, but now the sun emerged in splendour from behind the clouds. There was sunshine on the window. It confirmed Squeak's suspicion of the specialness of the air therein, which glittered, giving light back to the sun as water does. She looked again more closely at it, and saw that the tenants were not alone.

There was a bird with them. It was similar in most ways to the birds of the loft, but less substantial. She took a step to one side along the exterior ledge of the windowsill, and the bird moved with her; a step to the other, and it was with her again. It seemed to Squeak (though this must have been an illusion) that she could actually see through the bird, but it was there; it gazed back at her. Its intention was clear, to defend the tenants against her intrusion.

Every signal told Squeak that this bird was hostile to her. These facts, then, were to be considered. It was a bird, and not, as Squeak herself was, a tenant. It was hostile to Squeak. Yet it was permitted to be indoors, on Squeak's territory, with tenants whom Squeak was courting, when Squeak herself was excluded.

Her revenge must be terrible. She flew back to the patio wall to give herself a good start, took a moment's preparation, then launched herself against the kitchen window with as much force as she could muster. No prayers were said, no ritual offerings made; she went alone against calamity, like a Kamikaze pilot, beautiful and doomed. And at first it seemed as if fortune was with her. As she flew from the wall, the sun went behind a cloud again. The air in the window no longer glistened. She would get through.

She failed. The pain was extreme, her sense of loss and shame almost too great to be borne. The tenants had thought that she would crack the windowpane, then feared that she had cracked herself. At the moment of impact they were already halfway out of the kitchen, chairs falling behind them. They picked her up. They examined her gently. She allowed herself to be held and carried. It was attention of a sort, and at least the strange bird was gone.

'Nothing broken. I don't know why not.'

They could not mate with a bird; they must know that. Like could only mate with like, and it was their destiny to mate with her, as hers to mate with one of them. Squeak had accepted her own destiny. How long would the tenants obstinately contrive to evade theirs?

She had won a battle. Nobody won the war. She was no longer excluded from the inside of the house, was permitted to remain with the tenants throughout the day while they were in residence, and even to bathe with them as so long before. When they were absent, whether in London or Leamington, she bore their absence equably, and waited for them at the attic window; it is rejection, and not absence, which wounds a loving heart. She called to them, mostly from the oven glove, sometimes from a bathmat or the battered Numda rug in the study, for a while from the loft itself, when she found a promising place for a nest, protected by a sheet of plywood and an old fishing-net. Often they answered, as best they could, picking her up, petting her, talking to her, offering her hemp – *oh, comfort me with apples, for I am sick of love*. She showed to them, crouched, spread wings and lifted tail, lowered her head into their sad useless hands. They caressed her beak between fingers, gently scratched the plumage of her breast and neck: it was not enough, but it was all they could give her. They continued to speak of her as 'he'.

So might the unconsummated love affair between Squeak and the tenants have dragged its slow length through summer and into autumn and winter, becoming in its way like those human marriages in which pity takes the place of passion, and valleys which might have grown fertile are sown only with the salt of tears. But in the first fortnight of September, when blackberries and elder ripen in the hedges, and the purple aubretia has its second flowering, Squeak began to gather twigs, leaves and pieces of straw, picked at the tips of antirrhinums, and flew busily backwards and forwards from patio to attic with her trophies. This seemed like desperate behaviour to the tenants, and they grieved over it, for it indicated what they knew to be untrue, that Squeak and a partner had together chosen a home, mated, and were now furnishing against the arrival of little ones.

'He thinks he·can do it all himself,' a tenant said. 'He's given up on us, poor little bugger.'

This was the tenant who, two days later, on the morning on 13 September, found Squeak behind the plywood and the fishing-net, crouching amid a litter of nesting materials which included, as was discovered, the discarded skin of rhubarb, and warming what was undeniably an egg.

FIVE

Monster

AT LAST the tenants had discovered that Squeak was a hen, and there is no longer any need in this narrative to make disconcerting switches of gender so as to accommodate the points of view of both Squeak and the tenants. Just as once they had accepted the fact that she was a London pigeon it seemed extraordinary to them that they have ever believed her to be anything else, so now it became clear to them that Squeak had always been a hen. She was small and anxious, affectionate and faithful, intelligent and inventive, while cocks are a stupid and promiscuous lot, insensitive and inconsiderate in their

88

behaviour (they had already forgotten the Fantail).

Squeak had laid an egg; in a couple of days she would lay another. Both eggs would be infertile, since she had no mate. Impregnation by a male bird is not essential to the laying of eggs; it is an emotional matter, a response to pairing, and clearly Squeak believed that she had paired with them. It was not unknown, nor even uncommon, for hens secluded in their own sub-division of the loft, to form attachments to each other (as the Cream had done before succumbing to inflammation of the brain) and then both hens would lay infertile eggs, four in all, and attempt to hatch them if they were not removed. Wilf and Wendell had never laid eggs; they had the disposition for it, but lacked the apparatus. But all hens laid eggs. Even Barbara Cartland had managed one.

The tenants discussed the morality and the practicality of allowing Squeak to try to hatch eggs which they themselves knew to be infertile. The morality was over the question of deception, and did not detain them long; it is not a mortal sin to deceive a pigeon, nor was direct deceit involved, but merely a decision not to correct error. The practicality was more complicated. As long as Squeak remained sitting on infertile eggs, she was not inducing guilt in the tenants by displaying her lovelorn condition all over the house and garden, obliging them constantly to witness what they could not alleviate. When, after eighteen days or so, the eggs had not hatched, she would abandon them, and perhaps lay again, and resume her sitting. It was a situation devoutly to be wished, contenting both parties, but for the fact that Squeak had no partner to take turns with her. She would be unable to leave the eggs to eat, drink, or take exercise – which is to say that she would in fact have to leave them, but unwillingly and for the shortest periods of time, so that she would, by the end of this period of abortive hatching, have become weak and undernourished.

Might not the tenants prevent this unhappy conclusion by placing food and water within her reach? They might, they would, but it would have to be in open containers of white plastic, such as are commonly secured to the sides of nestboxes and carrying cases. Plywood and a fishing-net do not offer the same attachments; the water would easily be tipped over, and the food become fouled. As long as the tenants were in residence, the food and water could be restored to prime condition twice a day, but while they were away . . . The tenants concluded that, while they were away, Squeak would have to manage as best she could.

She sat obsessively. She would not leave the eggs. The tenants, a couple susceptible at any time to slights, saw in the intensity of her devotion a reproach to themselves. They came sheepishly to the loft, sat on their hams by the fishing-net, and gentled her. She took this attention as her right, nibbled at their fingers with her beak, ate hemp, small grains and peanuts graciously from the hands of tenants in danger of falling over, the muscles of whose thighs were sending urgent messages of pain. On the first of such visits, clearly believing that she was about to be relieved on the nest, she had stood, moved away a little, and seemed inclined for a snack and a constitutional. The tenant, feeling it to be the least that one could do in such a case, had placed a hand over the eggs to keep them warm in her absence. Squeak had seen at once that this would not be enough. She had returned, pushed the hand out of the way, and settled herself as before to wait out the hatching.

Well, they were poor things; she knew that by now. She would take from them such help and comfort as was offered, but would expect nothing, depend on none beyond herself. She was not surprised when, one morning, after a visit, accompanied by incoherent noises and the offer of special food, she heard the car start, and they did not return for some days.

During the four days they were away, the water dish tipped over and so did the dish of small grains, which were wetted by the water and became unpalatable. Squeak sat, thirsty, in the wet, and warmed her eggs. The rhubarb skin rotted, and the soggy grains were fouled by droppings. She picked amongst garbage, and took from it what nourishment she could. She was noticeably thinner when the tenants returned, and her eyes were bright like those of a man in fever. The tenants offered her fresh water, and she dipped her beak into the dish and drank copiously. They offered her small grains, and she ate voraciously. They attempted to clean under and around her, but this was a threat to the eggs, and was resisted.

'It's no good. We'll have to take them away. She can't stay like this.' Other hens of the loft had laid eggs anyhow in corners, sat for a while in a slipshod way, and left them to grow cold, fertile or no. Squeak's devotion was total. She would waste away in this attempt to hatch infertile eggs; the irony was too bitter to savour. A tenant moved one hand gently beneath her, and was allowed, without so much as a wing flap, to take an egg, watched by Squeak. The egg was held up against the bare bulb of the electric light, a process known as 'candling'. It was fertile.

Return of the egg. Withdrawal of tenants. The moral and practical discussion resumed.

So she had been covered, and had not noticed it.

Certainly she had formed no attachment as a result of it. The tenants looked about, like Victorian parents, for a culprit. Would it have happened while they had so unwisely penned her with the cocks? Had Ginge been at his tricks again? But there was no point to such speculation: shot-gun weddings are inapplicable to the world of pigeons. Whichever cock bird had covered Squeak would already have forgotten doing so, and she, it must be assumed, had not even noticed what was happening, being entirely consumed by her passion for the tenants themselves. She had shrugged off, perhaps, her over-importunate admirer, but, being abstracted, had done so a little after the event. Now it was too late to find a father. While she sat, while she hatched, while she reared the pair of nestlings, no bird would pair with her, nor she with any.

While she hatched, while she reared – no, it could not be allowed. Squeak was a single parent. The tenants had seen already the emaciation, the ill health brought about by their leaving her for four days with only herself to feed, because she would not leave the eggs. Imagine the eggs hatched, imagine a couple of importunate squeakers, reaching at all times into her crop to take from it what she had only with difficulty managed to put in, all the nourishment going to them, while Squeak slowly starved. There were sound social reasons in this case for the avian equivalent of abortion, which is to take the eggs, fertile or no, and throw them in the field for magpie, crow or weasel.

And yet, though common sense and common humanity, in the person of one of the tenants, pointed one way, common humanity and common sense, in the person of the other, pointed another. Squeak had already shown herself to have the instincts of a devoted mother. When she had endured so much in caring for her eggs, was it kind, was it fair, was it wise simply to throw them away? Leave aside the question of possible psychological damage, since so little is known of the psychology of pigeons, there still remained the question of Squeak's own future *as a pigeon*. There could be no doubt that, imprinted as she was, she believed that she would hatch a tenant. For her own sake as one who must, if she were to find her own fulfilment, make a pair-bond with another bird, it would be wiser to let her hatch the eggs and rear the chicks, making her own discovery that what had come out of her own body, the beings of which she was undeniably the mother, were birds, not tenants. By that she would know herself to be a bird also, and so the power of the imprint would be broken, and Squeak would no longer call importunately from an oven glove or hurl herself against the kitchen window for love's sake.

It was decided that one egg should be taken, one left in the nest. To feed and rear two chicks would be beyond the capacity of any single pigeon, but Squeak, with a little help from her friends, should be able to manage one. She would experience the joys of motherhood, and she would make an important discovery about herself.

Squeak allowed one egg to be taken, just as earlier she had allowed one to be removed for candling. It is possible that she still believed that the tenants would accept their parental obligations, and that to relieve her of the responsibility of one egg might be their way of doing so. She watched, but did not prevent or pursue; she sat on. The egg was thrown into the field, and had gone by morning. The remaining egg, in its time, pipped, and produced a blind, naked nestling to be cherished by Squeak.

The provision of food and water was not, in fact, a problem, as the tenants should have known. Naked nestlings, even at the very beginnings of their lives, do not require the obsessive sitting given by parent birds to a pair of eggs, once the second has been laid. They are subject to cold, but do not, at least in early autumn, expire of hypothermia if left uncovered for a minute or so, and since the nest was concealed from the main traffic of the loft by plywood, Squeak's chick was not likely to be killed by other birds. When Squeak required food and water she ate and drank with her fellows, and returned at once to feed the chick. Which grew.

It squeaked; it fed. It put on yellow down. It opened its eyes. It fed; it squeaked. It pushed its head into its mother's mouth, and received the cheesy substance which is called crop milk. Quills pushed out from inside its skin. Crop milk gave way to partially digested grains. It sat up in the nest, regarding its small world incuriously when it was not eating or squeaking. Squeak sat sometimes on and sometimes beside it.

The tenants decided that, although it could not be a bird of pedigree, they would band one leg with one of the National Pigeon Association's rings, in part out of compliment to Squeak, but also so that they would always be able to tell its age. At a week old, a chick's bones are flexible. Three toes pressed together, the fourth drawn back impossibly over the leg, to lie flat against it, and so the ring was slipped over all four, to remain in place when the fourth toe was permitted to resume its usual position. Squeak watched. So it went.

Feathers appeared from the quills, though bare patches of skin remained around the eyes and under the wings. The bird would be white – well, mainly white; most of the feathers were white. That put Ginge in the clear. The colouring became more apparent as the feathers grew more numerous and closer together. Yellow down persisted on its head, but the bird would certainly be white, although interestingly marked. Would it, the tenants wondered, have inherited Squeak's intelligence? If it were male, would it make a suitable mate for her? Such incestuous pairings were common among the Pharaohs, and they are common among pigeons. The chick continued to grow. It was fed on demand devotedly by Squeak, and it grew at a great rate. It would be a large bird.

The markings, if one had to describe them, were as though someone had spilled brown ink on the bird, and wiped it off clumsily. Considered over a period, they were not so much interesting as ugly. Furthermore, feathers were sprouting from the feet. Squeak's squab would be muffed, like Mr Carpet Slippers. There were several muffed birds in the Main Loft. A large bird. Muffed. The tenants' gaze turned towards Bully Boys One and Two, the delinquent Saxon Shields, great lumpish hobbledehoys, white of body, their feet clumsily feathered. The shields on their wings were light brown, the colour of spilled ink. Their father, Mr Saxon, had been given away to an auctioneer, who had admired him at the Flower Show. As he had not been seen about the village since, the tenants believed that he had ended as pigeon pie or in a pet shop. Now that he was gone, the two Bully Boys were all that remained of that family. They had inherited none of their father's stockbrokerly airs. One could not imagine them at Stationers' Hall; they belonged in a back kitchen, twisting their caps between their hands. They could not endure the tenants' suspicious gaze, and flapped away, as ungainly as pelicans.

A large bird, an ugly bird, clumsy and ill-proportioned. He was already larger than his mother. He squeaked and pursued her, and still she fed him. She could hardly eat enough to keep them both alive, but he saw no reason to pick for himself when it was more convenient to be fed. The tenants were reminded of Aldous Huxley's story of the noble dwarf, Sir Hercules, and his dwarf lady, who conceived a child of normal height. They decided to call the squab 'Monster'. Sir Hercules' son had set his parents on a table and thrown walnuts at them. If they saw anything of that kind of behaviour from Monster, he would be rapidly dealt with.

As for Squeak, from the time of laying she had given up the life of intelligence and reason for that of emotion and instinct, and was content that this should be so because instinct told her that it was always so. Intelligence and reason must be subordinate now to motherhood, first to hatching and then feeding. One laid an egg, and kept it warm. In time, a being emerged from it, and this being continued to require warmth and also food, which must be provided on demand. As more time passed, the demand for warmth diminished, and that for food increased. The being made signals to indicate when it required food; it squeaked, and agitated its body, whereupon one opened one's mouth, and the being thrust in its head, and took food. Even when it was not eating, it demanded the reassurance of one's near presence, and one gave it that reassurance, sitting at first on or partly on it, later by it. If it should be attacked, one defended it. If it were unhappy, one comforted it.

It grew. It was bigger than she. Its appetite began to become difficult to satisfy, and the presence of its beak inside her own mouth painful, as was the perpetual pumping-up of partially digested grains from her crop. There was not enough food in the world for the two of them. She made the experiment of refusing to feed it when next the being demanded food. It attacked her. Astonished, she flew up to a perch near the roof, while the being squeaked below her. Intelligence and reason, those old friends, were back at her wingtips. The feeling heart which had governed her actions for so long grew harder. Instinct and emotion, strong as they would always be and dear to her, resumed their proper places in the direction of Squeak's life, and sweet reason ruled again. She looked down at the squeaker. It was nothing like herself and the tenants. It resembled the birds in the loft, but was ill-formed even by their standards. It was a monster, which had invaded the nest she had made for herself. She descended, and drove it out, while it squeaked dismally.

Well, pigeons do drive away their offspring, usually when the hen has laid again and the eggs are about to hatch, and within a month the three will meet as strangers. So it goes. Monster wandered forth into the Main Loft, where he was chased about by several birds, but was too large to be bullied. There were food and water in containers, and now that this knowledge demanded application, he discovered that he knew very well how to feed himself. He found a perch on top of the inner door. It was the least satisfactory perch in the Main Loft since, whenever the inner door was closed, it ceased to exist, but it was traditionally the perch for new arrivals, and it did for Monster.

Like all the young birds, he soon found his way to the window. Curiosity, or a push from some bird behind, took him out on to the roof. He had the usual difficulty in finding his way back in the evening, but once he had discovered the connection between them, both worlds, of indoors and outdoors, were his. The tenants looked sourly up from the patio, watched him clownishly navigating the gutter, picking out for degustation who knew what piece of filth, and wished that Squeak had been more choosy.

'You wouldn't say he looks a little like Jean-Louis Barrault in *Les Enfants du Paradis*?'

'No.'

'Maybe not.'

Squeak had returned to the tenants, but there was a difference. She preferred their company to that of the birds in the loft, but she no longer offered love. She had been grossly deceived. Such wounds are slow to heal. Later, if the inclination to mate grew strong in her again, she might be driven to offer herself, since there was practically speaking no other choice, but for the time being she and the tenants would remain just friends. She would use their heads as watchtowers, travel upon their shoulders like a mahout upon an elephant, take hemp, peanuts and tares graciously from their hands. From time to time, in a platonic way, she would nibble the lobe of an ear or test the tensile strength of a fingernail with her beak, but no more. She would not crouch. She would not nod her head.

For the tenants it was a most welcome return to what had been. Time passes, they reminded each other, and the agonies of love recede into memory, becoming a little shabby there, a little ridiculous. Friendship is what lasts, friendship between pigeon and tenant, based on mutual toleration, mutual respect, mutual support. (What support did Squeak give to the tenants? She assisted them towards a good opinion of themselves. One can't be much more supportive than that.) As for Monster, well they were landed with him, but the tenants were well accustomed to mismarked and unshowable birds. He would get no special privileges, and must rub along as well as he could.

In the garden, the bergamot was in flower, and the heavy-headed sedum was covered with gluttonous bees and Purple Emperors. Wasps harvested the richness of yellow plums, and the peaches, gathered hastily in to save them from a similar fate, were found to be infested with earwigs, and fit only for chutney. Runner beans grew vast and stringy more quickly than they could be picked. The freezer, newly filled, hummed to itself in the woodshed.

Log fires were lit in the evenings, and there was speculation as to when the still-flowering geraniums should be brought indoors. The first frost came, and the leaves of the dogwood were flushed with pink.

The tenants had been spending as little time in London as they could, making small forays to pick up mail, attend some few necessary meetings, show their faces at the centre of affairs in order to maintain a place there, since it is the nature of the centre that faces seldom shown are soon forgotten. This had been done out of necessity, and reluctantly; they would sooner have stayed where they were, stretching out a summer of sunny days. Frost restored them to a more proper sense of reality; they remembered how easy it is to drop off the tree. On the Monday after the frost, they loaded the boot of the car with the produce of their garden (some to be consumed by themselves in South Kensington, some to be given away to reluctant friends, who had their own gardens, their own tomatoes, their own beans, most of all their own rhubarb) and set off. They would return at the weekend; that was the way of it in winter. Squeak stood on the gatepost, and watched them go.

The car turned the corner halfway up the track, and was lost to sight though she could still hear it. She left the gatepost and flew to the top of the bird table. She was free; she had choice. Grains of maize had been scattered on the patio by the tenants as a parting gift to any who might wish to accept it. The only accepters so far were two sparrows and a chaffinch, but if Squeak flew down, they would fly away. Squeak considered the maize and the three small beings hopping about among it. She did not wish maize. If she wished, she might fly about the house, making wide circles in the air for the joy of it, pushing down into the valley, then turning upwards towards the woods, over-flying her whole territory, flapping her wings so that they touched at the top, gliding, turning, swerving, feeling the air like liquid over her wings, then landing on the chimney or the ridge of the roof to rest before, if she were in the flying mood, taking off again. Yes, she might fly; often she did; later she would. Or she might return to her own chosen place by the fishing-net and the plywood, and remain there until it was time to eat. Or she might do as she already was doing, which was to remain where she was, considering her options.

Few of the birds were out. Once pushed out by the tenants, and denied re-entry by the closing of the plastic trellis, they would behave as if the roof and the patio were their natural place until the cool of evening set them to an agitated fluttering and crowding of the windowledge. But in truth, left to themselves, they preferred for most of the time to remain indoors, where they conducted a perpetual committee meeting, puffing out their chests and interrup-

100

ting each other, jumping up to put dubious points of order and information, losing the agenda, dropping into and out of sleep, indulging in private conversation (much of it scandalous) and petty disloyalties – pigeons were born for the House of Commons, and it is no wonder that so many may be found in Parliament Square. So that now, left to themselves by the departing tenants, most of the mature birds had resumed the Committee Stage of the Main Loft Amelioration Bill, and only a few young birds, not yet sure of a seat, were out to take the air. Amongst these was Monster.

An ugly bird; a greedy bird. He stood on the gutter and thrust his neck forwards, measuring the flight to the maize below. Squeak had already forgotten that he was her child, and he no longer pursued her, squeaking. He could get food for himself; he could drive away other pigeons from food he fancied, lumbering against them like a dinosaur. He launched himself from the gutter, landed clumsily, then addressed himself seriously to the grains of maize. Another young bird, a well-feathered Grizzle, followed him down.

It was a clear cold day. Squeak looked across at the valley, at bullocks in one field, sheep in another, at a line of telegraph poles marching down to distant buildings, and smoke rising from those buildings. All was as it should be. Soon she would decide what she most wished to do, and then she would do it. A magpie flew out of the wood. She cocked her head, and looked up at the sky. Something was up there, high and hovering. The chatter of sparrows in the clematis suddenly ceased, and all the birds of the wood were silent.

The something dropped out of the air. The young Grizzle rose, terrified, from the patio, and began to fly wildly about the house, joined by the other young birds who had been on

101

the roof. Squeak discovered that she had left the bird table, and was in the wisteria which covered the front of the house, hiding among the leaves. She did not know how she had reached the wisteria, but knew she could not leave it, not for any nice reasons of calculation, but because her body would not move from it, could only cling to it. The something which had come out of the air was now at rest on the patio. It held Monster in its claws.

It was a bird, a large bird, larger than any bird of the loft, not of her own kind, not of the tenants'. It had a hooked grey beak at the end of its flat grey head, in which the mad eyes were set further forward than her own or those of the birds of the loft. Its back was roughly the colour of the kitchen table, and its long grey tail was like a ladder, barred with black. It held Monster securely, crouching over him. Monster was alive, but did not struggle; he was rigid with fear. The bird began to use its beak to tear out first the feathers and then the flesh of Monster's back.

Monster's eyes and beak were open. Pigeons, though they can complain and chide and coo, have no noise to express extremes of pain. The pigeons of the attic were silent also; their committee had gone into recess. Above the roof, the young birds still flew in circles, afraid to land, but tiring. The bird on the patio took no notice of them, being absorbed in its immediate business of eating Monster alive. One of the young birds made a clumsy landing on the slates, and scrambled its way back into the safety of the loft, quickly followed by its fellows. The grey bird did not even look up. Squeak remained where she was, and watched the bird eating. After some time, Monster shuddered and died. This was of no great consequence to the bird, which required its meat to be fresh, but not necessarily sentient; the suffering of another being was not a sauce to its own enjoyment. It ate on seriously, having reached Monster's viscera by way of his back.

Time passed. The pigeons in the wood began to converse among themselves again and from the bottom of the garden a blackbird chattered angrily. The pigeons of the loft remained silent. A crow arrived, and perched on the wooden fence at the end of the vegetable garden, where it was joined by its mate. The large bird took no notice of the crows, perhaps did not even see them; it did not fear crows. It paused in eating, and glanced up at the wisteria. Squeak discovered that she could, after all, move, and shrank even further into the cover of the leaves. Had it been possible to incorporate her being into the cement between the stones of the wall, she would have done so. The grey bird left Monster's body, walked to the bowl of drinking water kept on the patio for the refreshment of pigeons, and drank from it. It seemed no longer to be hungry. The two crows moved from the fence to the top of the garden wall, and waited. The grey bird took one step, then two across the patio, rose clumsily in the air, its claws trailing below it, and then flew, no longer clumsy, its pointed wings rising high above it, the long barred tail stretched out behind, cutting diagonally up into the air, above trees, above the line of telegraph poles, high over the church and the village, and was gone. The two crows moved in from the garden wall, and in the attic loft an intrepid pigeon reminded its honourable friends that the committee was still in session.

Time passed. Squeak remained where she was among wisteria. The two crows had their way with the leavings, and were joined by other crows. Some portions of

Monster's body were scattered and dispersed about the patio, some carried away to be consumed elsewhere. Time passed. Squeak might have left her shelter if she wished, and returned to her chosen place by the plywood and the fishing-net. She discovered that she did not wish to do so. She could hear the committee in full voice; its proceedings had never greatly concerned her, and did not do so now.

Where were the tenants? They had driven away in their noisy box, and allowed death to fall from the air. She had watched death eating. It had come for Monster, and might return at will for her. Nowhere was safe. She remained where she was.

Evening came. The air thickened, and its temperature dropped. The crows had finished their meal. The remnants of it would not feed five thousand, but a fox arrived, walking delicately up the drive, cocked its leg against a species rose, sniffed at and then inspected the remnants, and carried off a head from which the eyes had already been picked. All that was left of Monster was a bunch of feathers and the National Pigeon Association's yellow ring.

The wisteria was still young, not yet a tree, less than seven years old; it had never flowered. Its branches had length, but little width. A frightened bird might cling to any, but none would provide a comfortable resting place on which a bird might couch to sleep. It hugged the wall: Squeak had been glad enough that it did, but had become increasingly aware that the close proximity of stone left a bird no room to perch. Considered as a refuge, there was much to be said for the wisteria. Considered as a bed for the night, there was much it lacked.

She had been out of the loft too long, and the dark was gathering round her. She left the wisteria, but the outlines of roof, bird table, porch and patio wall were obscured and unfamiliar. Where the entrance to the loft should be was only darkness, and within the darkness only silence, for the committee never went into all-night sitting unless the tenants left the attic light on by accident. She flew up, she flew down again, and stood on the patio amid the murk, frightened and uncertain, for the patio was open to the sky and every sort of predator. In height was safety. Was the roof safe? From what went on four legs, yes, but death, as now she knew, came out of the air. Should she return to the uncomfortable safety of the wisteria? But it was only a darkness now against the wall of the house. There was a pale shape, something large on great wings, moving silently at about the height of the roof but beyond the garden gate. She flew wildly towards where she knew the bird table to be, and struck one of the wooden struts which held up its roof with her wing. She grabbed wildly at the edge of the table with her claws, and pulled herself on to it, safely under the shelter of its roof, settling herself amongst the husks of wild-bird food and old sunflower seeds. Something moved on the patio. And out in the field, in the direction taken by the flying shape, a rabbit screamed.

Something moved on the patio. She heard the feet, very faintly, and strained to see. As she moved forward a little on the bird table, turning her head towards the sound, the movement ceased. She had heard the something, and it had heard her. Both were silent, both still.

It was the night, a time not to confront danger but to have already removed oneself from any possibility of it. For hundreds of years, woodpigeons and rock doves had roosted in trees and on the sides of cliffs. The feral pigeons who were Squeak's more immediate ancestors on her father's side had taken to ledges, gutters, clock towers and the statues of celebrated persons, and slept safe in the crook of some marble arm. On her mother's side, generations of Chinese Owls had been protected by structures of wood and wire netting variously sited in the back gardens of the Fancy.

She could see nothing; she could hear nothing. She reminded herself that she was above ground; the something would not be able to reach her, even if it intended her harm. From beyond the edge of the dark woods the top of a wan moon cast a glimmer of light on to the patio, where it was dimly reflected from the slabs of composition stone with which the patio was covered. There was a darkness against the stone; this something had come to glean what remained of the maize. It had a long body, and a tail as long. It was an animal, furred not feathered.

The animal raised its head, and looked up at the bird table. The moonlight glittered in its eyes and on the white of teeth. Squeak shrank back among the husks, the unwanted seeds and what had once been bacon rinds.

She was above ground, well above ground, and beneath cover. She had chosen well. No bird of the air, no beast of the field could come against her.

The bird table did not, of course, rest upon a cushion of air, like some spacecraft upon an alien planet. It had been bought by mail order from the Royal Society for the Protection of Birds, had arrived unsupported in a cardboard box, and had then been set up in the lower part of the front garden on a stout pole, which was a trimmed sapling of larch from the woods above the house. It is doubtful whether Squeak recognized the function of this pole. Recognition of function in pigeons is usually limited to such necessary matters as that food containers may be assumed to contain food and plastic bowls the water for baths. The animal, however, appeared to have a clear sense of function, or at least of the paths which must be taken, the methods adopted, in order to reach what is desired. Squeak watched the darkness of its body move across the patio and the eyes appear at the top of the low wall which bordered that part of the garden. Then that darkness was lost to sight amongst vegetation and against the darker earth.

It had looked up at her. It had moved towards her. Now she could no longer see it.

The dark creature was by now directly below the bird table at the base of the pole. It put out a paw, and tested the security of the pole, and also that its surface was not too smooth to climb. Then it began the ascent.

Squeak felt the faintest of tremors beneath her. She heard the faintest of scratching of claws on wood. Every instinct instructed her to shrink to the very centre of the table, where she would be most protected both from above and below. These instincts were responding to an extreme of fear. 'Hide!' they said, 'Crouch!', just as earlier they had taken her, quicker than thought, into the shelter of the wisteria. But this time the approach of danger was more gradual, and fear spoke not only to instinct, but to intelligence, and with a different voice, advising Squeak that if she were to resist the danger, she must discover its nature and the nature of its approach. Such contradictory instructions may induce a total paralysis of the will. They did not do so in Squeak. She forced herself to the edge of the bird table, and looked over and down. Darkness flowed up the pole towards her, following its own glittering eyes.

It is possible that the large brown rat which was climbing so expertly towards her would have been defeated at having to travel the last stage of its journey upside down horizontally across the base of the bird table, but I would not lay money on it. Certainly Squeak was not disposed to hazard her own life on such a chance. She took off like an Exocet missile, and flew through moonlight to the pitchy darkness of the woods.

She knew trees, and had been in the woods once before. She did not remember the occasion, but it had occurred. The tenants had grown ambitious, and had extended a walk through fields to a bridle path which ran through the woods to the west. Squeak, safe passenger upon a shoulder, had taken a whim to leave it, found flight obstructed by branches, and had perched twenty feet above the head of a fretful tenant, who remained on the path below, stretching out arms and uttering the mysterious noises the tenants did usually make when she was out of reach in some strange place – or, if you should prefer the tenants' version, calling, 'Squeak! Come on, Squeakie! Here, Squeak! Oh, for Christ's sake, come on, you stupid bird; I can't stand here all afternoon.'

She knew trees, but not these trees, and not in the dark. She had taken off without consciously choosing a direction; she had put distance between herself and danger. Branches had brushed against her; she had not minded them. She had flown through the pale darkness of moonlight into a deeper darkness, crowded with obstacles to flight, and had come to rest on something solid which was above ground. She did not know what lay below her, or how far below was. She concluded, as her wits resumed their function, that the objects above her which obscured the moon constituted some sort of cover. She would remain where she was.

All around there were noises in the darkness. Had she been capable of making such connections, she might have recognized some of these noises as nearer and louder versions of those which could be heard on any night from outside the loft. Couched between plywood and a fishing-net, drifting cosily in and out of sleep, one does not heed such noises; now she was part of them, lost among them, maybe prey to them. From below and at some distance there was a high screaming into which was mixed a yelping sound, but all, it seemed, as if from the same creature, caught in a trap and tearing its own body to pieces in an effort to recover its freedom. She could not know that it was the love-play of foxes, a little early in the year – for with foxes it is not the life-giving sun but cold which arouses desire. For Squeak the noise said, 'Fear! Pain! Danger!'

From her own level, again at some distance not to be judged, she heard the sleepy challenge and response of some sylvan committee-member. Well, that was reassurance. There were birds here, then, just as in the loft; it was not a place of total strangeness. But as if in answer to the honourable member, there suddenly burst out the most angry whirring noise, also from her own level, as if a lawnmower had developed wings and a will of its own, and lay in wait among the larches, terrible in wrath, seeking whom it might devour.

Below, a snapping of twigs, something large moving through brambles. Noises on all sides, both up and down, merging into each other, then suddenly distinct, but never silent. Even the solid object on which she rested, and others like it in the dark around her, even the protective cover above was not still, but creaked and moved. These solids were alive, and talked among themselves. The very air was not still. It moved both itself and the branches, crying out like some sick thing, unable to rest or settle.

And far above, one thin cry, cutting through all the other noises of the dark, silencing the lawnmower and the honourable members, the birds roosting in branches and the animals below, even for a moment, as it seemed, the wind and the moving branches. One thin cry, and then in the distance another, and then no more, whereat the night noises resumed in all their dangerous diversity.

She could not sleep, and must not. She must stay where she was, and wait out the dark. There was nowhere left to go, all places being equally perilous, even if she could have seen her way. No, it was time to stand. If anything more solid than the wind were to approach, she had a beak, she had wings to flap against it; she was not defenceless. If either of the tenants had been by, they would have remembered Alphonse Daudet's courageous little goat – *et puis, dans le matin, le loup lui mangea* – but Squeak lacked the consolations of a grammar school education. She did not need them. *Adieu, Alphonse!* She would not close her eyes.

Time passed. The wind dropped, and rain began to fall. At first she heard only the pattering on the leaves above her, and looked up in dread of what creature might be making it. Then the rain broke through. Squeak's feathers became soggy. She could not fly now, even if she would. She closed her eyes, and slept, and awoke to the dawn.

All about her was the most tremendous din, and she recognized it as the dawn chorus. Often before, on hearing it, she had left the loft, and gone forth to peck among the gravel of the drive, searching for grit, but also for the seeds of weeds; although food was to be had for the taking in the loft, it was sometimes dismally nutritious – linseed or pigeon pellets – and a free spirit likes to forage for itself. The rain had stopped. She flapped her wings to dry them, and could hear (but not see) other birds doing the same. She dipped her beak into the oil glands at the base of her tail, and began to anoint her feathers.

She was hungry. She would not spurn linseed now, or pigeon pellets if they were offered.

Squeak was within thirty yards of the edge of the wood above the house, though her view of it was obstructed by trees. It is possible that she still associated danger with the direction from which she had come, and was reluctant to return. In any case, birds near her, whom she recognized by their conversation as close kin to the birds of the loft, were beginning to move another way, and she went with them.

There was a field of barley above the woods at the top of the hill. The crop had been harvested, but grain for the taking had been spilled in the stubble. Squeak's knowledge of fields was confined to the four between which the house was set and over which she had often flown, and, in a theoretical way as a distant prospect, to those which lay in the valley before and beyond the village. She had never been to the top of the hill, except in transit, confined in a box in the car; the single occasion described earlier had taught the tenants not to trust her in woods. Now she came out of the woods to the north-east, and found a flock of woodpigeons gleaning barley. It seemed to her that danger of most sorts would be diminished if she were to place herself among them. With so many larger birds to choose from, why should a predator take Squeak? The middle of the flock would be best. And she was, as has been observed, hungry.

So Squeak lived for four days among the pigeons of the woods, moving with the flock, eating grain, seeds and small berries, and drinking from puddles. A sudden noise, the shadow of a hang-glider or helicopter over the hill, even an unexpected fracas amongst rooks would start them, and they would rise in a flock, Squeak among them, circle, then settle again. When they returned to the trees, she would be with them. They were bigger than she. If she were to approach too close to any, it might chase her away; otherwise she was ignored. At night she roosted alone in a tree. She made no attempt to find again the patio, the bird table, the drive with its necessary grit, the plastic baths and the water bowl, the loft and all its community; it was as if she had forgotten them. She began to distinguish between the noises of the night, not to know what caused them, but to judge how far away they were, how far below or above, how threatening. With this knowledge, she slept more easily, though always lightly.

Early during the fourth night, she heard a different sound, a roaring which she recognized. She heard it approaching, knew its destination, moved as quickly as she could from branch to branch towards it. She reached the lower edge of the wood as the noise ceased, and the two giant eyes of the creature which made the noise lost their brightness and disappeared.

The tenants closed the doors of their car, and stumbled through the darkness towards the garden gate, carrying their usual litter of briefcases and carrier-bags. There came from the edge of the woods a dark bird, flying. They did not see it, heard perhaps the beating of wings, but did not apprehend it. The bird came suddenly to them out of the night, aiming for the lightest mark it could see, which was the face of the nearer tenant, and changed direction sharply at the very last moment so as to avoid a collision. Both tenants cried out, and the nearer tenant dropped a carrier-bag containing free-range eggs, which broke. Squeak's claws skidded across the tenant's scalp, but she was on familiar ground, and did not overshoot the landing-strip. She gripped the tenant's hair securely and settled herself on the head to be carried indoors.

SIX

A Kind of Ending

It was worse than before. She would not leave them.

They could not know what had happened or when, but knew that something had happened, and that it must have been of a terrifying nature to drive Squeak from the loft to roost outdoors.

They discovered that Monster was missing. No other birds had gone. There was no sign of damage to the loft. From this small and mainly negative base of fact, speculation must, like some sea creature of indeterminate and adjustable shape, push outwards, testing and trying what it could find in the way of food.

114

There was an owl, often to be seen of an evening, looking out from the broken window of an adjacent barn. It would sit there, framed in the window, gazing amiably at the tenants across the barnyard, as if Thomas Bewick before his death had told it not to budge and had forgotten to rescind the instruction. The tenants had never seen the owl in flight, but it must fly, must hunt to live. They consulted books, as they so often did. Voles, mice, the tiny animals of the night are prey to owls. Monster had not been tiny, and would not have been out at night.

There was a cat, black with yellow eyes, wild as far as was known, which was to be observed sometimes at a distance, hunting among the rabbit burrows at the edge of the woods, and had once been found in the vegetable garden, couched in ambush among onions. The tenants had believed that any cat which believed that it could be hidden by onions was unlikely to endanger their pigeons, but they had chased it away, and when last seen it had been limping.

Not the owl, not likely to have been the cat. Was there a stoat again? But the pigeons, as has been remarked earlier, had taken their own precautions against the stoat by moving long ago to the attic. Rats? Harvest mice had come indoors for the warm during the tenants' first winter, had lived on and among the foam rubber which insulated the water pipes, and had been heard at night, skittering between floors. Consequently there might still be found in odd places forgotten traps, some still baited with mouldering hazelnuts, others containing mummified mice. The tenants did not forget the mice, and were mightily afraid that rats would one day come inside the house also, following a trail of corn from the patio by devious ways to the attic. Rats would make a massacre in the loft. But there had been no massacre, no deaths at all, only the disappearance of Monster and the flight of Squeak. The tenants searched for rat-droppings, and found none. Speculation had done with the rats. There were no rats.

Early next morning, a tenant saw from a bedroom window one brown rat, feeding on the patio, and shot it.

But it was not the rat. If Monster had been very greedy or very careless, if he had been caught in a sudden rainstorm which had so drenched his feathers that he could not fly, a rat might have caught him (as might the cat, however ill-concealed by onions), but that would not account for Squeak's departure. The sea creature, Speculation, pushing out antennae, contorting its gelatinous body in various directions, found no nourishment of hard facts, withered and died. Meanwhile there was the problem of Squeak.

She had been taken to the attic, and left there. At first light next morning, she was at the bedroom window, tapping on the glass. Allowed to enter, she settled on the end of the bed, and remained there until the rising of the tenants, when she partook of muesli, and accompanied one of them to the bath. She did not, as she had when young, bathe with the tenant, but remained on the washbasin as an observer. Returned thereafter to the attic by one tenant, she left immediately by way of the window, made a swift reconnaissance of all rooms from outside, located the other tenant washing up, and was tapping for admittance again.

The tenants conferred, and decided that latitude must be allowed, at least for a while. Squeak had been, for whatever reason, upset, and had regressed emotionally to a state in which she needed the reassurance of company, the

116

company of those who had once been the source of all comfort and security, her parents, themselves. In the short term, therefore, she must be given immediate support, while the tenants worked out whatever ongoing therapy might seem appropriate to the long-term alleviation of her distress – which is to say that they hoped she would get over it by herself. The tenants never learned. They knew objectively that the application of reason, compassion and impeccably liberal principles had never yet achieved the New Jerusalem, even for human beings, but they persisted in attempting to apply these principles to Squeak, to whom they were even less applicable.

Even while the tenants conferred, the weather in Warwickshire turned around. Autumn winds stripped the leaves from wisteria and willow, hedge-maple, sycamore and ash. Curtains of rain came blowing up the valley from the south-west. All the bright flames which had clothed the trees were whipped away by wind and doused by rain. They lay soggily about lawn, rockery and flower beds, fell into the plastic bowls on the patio and lay there bleeding tannin into the pigeons' bath water; they floated for a while on the surface of the garden pool, before sinking to the mud at the bottom, there to decay and poison what fish had not been taken by the heron.

It was not a time for sitting out, but for indoor occupations. Chutney was to be made of green tomatoes, wine and jam from an excess of plums. Racing was to be watched on television of a Saturday afternoon, after the laying of small bets with Mr Beard, the bookie of Shipston-on-Stour. (He is no longer in business there, alas, though certainly not bankrupted by the tenants: a new Betting Shop has been opened next to the Do-It-Yourself.) Books were to be read by the fire, and some written. In all these occupations, Squeak made up the company.

She watched, she plumed herself, scratched herself, perched on a knee, an arm, a head. She was no longer in love, made no nests; the oven glove was nothing now to her. Only she must be with them. Sometimes, when both were present, she would shift suddenly from one to the other, for no reason that could be guessed. Sometimes she would remove herself from both, and settle on the window seat or the back of the sofa. She did not look outside at the garden and the patio, as once she had been used to do; she watched only the tenants. When one tenant left the room, that did not disturb her; she would remain with the other. If both left, she would follow.

The tenants were unable to give themselves entirely to racing or to books, for their country home, they began to realize, was full of unanticipated perils. Squeak did not know what fire was, and had no fear of it. In one of her sudden shifts of ground, she might fly towards the inglenook, into smoke and flaming logs. She had no conception of the boiling-point of chutney, and would not keep a proper distance from the pan. What if she were to take a fancy to bathe in it? There was inconvenience also. One cannot housetrain a pigeon. *Harbinger Bird IV* could be wiped with a damp cloth, corduroy and denim laundered, but the expensive tweed which covered the sofa was another matter.

That week, when the tenants returned to London, they took Squeak with them. She had forgotten the flat, no longer recognized it as her territory; she was puzzled by it and alarmed by the low ceilings, against which she bumped when surveying these new boundaries. Should either tenant try to work at a desk, she picked neurotically at paper clips until the attempt was given up. Nor, when the tenants wished to leave the flat, or had invited others to visit it, did she take at all well to being confined in a cardboard box. What once had been security was now indignity. The cardboard cases in which Messrs Haynes, Hanson and Clark deliver their less expensive wines (and the more expensive also, for all the tenants knew) took a battering of wings. Water was spilled; wet grains trampled to a paste. Books placed on top flew off as by the action of a poltergeist. Nothing less weighty than a cast-iron frying-pan could keep Squeak down. Only the achievement of total darkness could silence her complaint. The tenants came quickly back from South Kensington that week.

Enough was enough. One could not be a slave to Squeak. The tenants reminded each other that emotional support may do harm as well as good. On the one hand it may alleviate loneliness and despair, on the other promote an ongoing dependence which, in the end, cripples both the supported and the supporter. The tenants could not, for Squeak's own sake, allow themselves to be crippled by her in any ongoing way. The time for short-term support was over; it had lasted at least a week. Now a process of transference must begin.

Transference to what? Well, clearly the only healthy relationship possible for Squeak would be a *mutually* supportive relationship with another pigeon.

Once again the tenants stood in the loft, looking over the cock birds, but although their own position was essentially the same, inasmuch as they were *in loco parentis* to Squeak, the intention had changed. They were no longer to discover a callous seducer, who must be bullied into doing the decent thing. This time they were to choose a mate, not a bird of pedigree (since no eggs could be allowed to hatch), but some humdrum rub-along good fellow, the avian equivalent of the Boy Next Door, into whose care they might safely confide a nervous daughter.

They chose a mismarked Owl of indifferent feathering and no obvious attachments. They placed him with Squeak in a cardboard box. There was an explosion in the box. It could not, even to the most optimistic ear, be construed as courting behaviour. A tenant lifted the flap at the top of the box cautiously, and tried to peer inside. He was struck in the face by a rocketing Chinese Owl, now even less well feathered, since many feathers remained in the box. The Owl bumped off the face of the tenant towards the window, made several attempts to fly through the glass, then dropped lumpishly to the windowledge, scuttled into a corner, and remained there cowering. The tenant put his hand into the box. Squeak first nibbled the fingers, then stood on the hand. She was lifted out of the box, and transferred herself to a shoulder. She ignored the mismarked Owl.

Clearly it was not going to be easy.

When Squeak was taken to the loft that night, the mismarked Owl, a bird equable enough in temperament up to then, removed himself from a perch near her fishing-net to a much less favoured position as far away from her as he could get, nor would he thereafter allow a tenant to approach him. His attitude was that of one of those princes who go out to fight the dragon, and get badly mauled; the king's daughter was not for him, and her father could keep his kingdom. Later he was given away to a lady in Leamington, who promised a quiet home with no cats. She had aspirations towards an aviary, and the mismarked Owl was to begin it.

Who for Squeak and how? Soon it would be time for London again.

Next morning the question was debated over the washing-up. Squeak, though she herself took no direct part in it, stood on the head of one tenant, adjusting her position so as to keep the other continually under observation.

Although pigeons cannot be house-trained, they do have a certain delicacy about fouling their own nests, and one may often see a nestbowl, clean in the centre but with the edges cemented to the floor of the nestbox by droppings. It is habitual (or perhaps instinctive) for a pigeon, even outside the nest, to take two or three steps backwards before shitting, and Squeak, feeling the moment upon her, now took those instinctive (or habitual) steps, so that the dropping avoided altogether the hair of the tenant on whose head she was standing, and ran instead neatly down his nose.

'Piss off, you loathsome bird!' the tenant said, and the flat of his hand knocked Squeak to the draining-board.

The other tenant gazed at him as at one who has struck a crippled child, and left the room.

'This bird will settle in the loft if it kills me,' the tenant said, gathered Squeak up, and took her upstairs.

How often a paternalistic government assumes power with the most benevolent intentions, so that not merely medical care, education, old-age pensions, museums, libraries and tours of Modern Dance groups, but justice, social equality, an uncensored press, all are provided by decree. Yet later this same benevolent paternalism, when wilfully thwarted by dissident minority groups, who attempt to turn liberty into licence and to subvert the state (the very fountain of all benefits), at first with infinite reluctance and in exceptional cases, thereafter with an acceleration fuelled by guilt and fear, becomes punitive, oppressive, vindictive and at last openly murderous. Just so had the concerned and caring attitude of at least one of the tenants towards Squeak been revealed for what it was, not liberal democracy, but odious tyranny.

The tenant carried Squeak into the loft. Hitherto the plastic trellis which could be fitted over the window had been used to keep pigeons out. All barriers have two sides. Today it would keep Squeak in. Let her work what explosions in the loft she would; the tenant would not heed them. Holding Squeak firmly in one hand, he fitted the trellis over the window, then loosed her and left her in the attic with never a backward glance.

Some pigeons were, in fact, outside – not many, since the roof on a foggy autumn day was not a resort of choice, but a few. Among them was Dickie, one of the hand-reared six who had first excited Squeak's jealousy, now unhappily paired to a flighty Black. It was a self-chosen pairing, since neither was showable. They had settled in a nestbox on the floor of the Main Loft, an unfavoured box on the window-wall, and there the Black, insofar as she received encouragement from unattached cock birds, put herself about, while Dickie stayed at home, sitting on the eggs she had laid ten days before. Sometimes she relieved him, but by no means for the periods of twelve hours laid down in the literature. For most of the incubation, Dickie sat on, snatching what time he could for food and exercise, not knowing that it was all wasted care, since the tenants would substitute pottery eggs for the real eggs before they hatched, and should have done so already.

One of those snatched times was now. Dickie was outside when the plastic trellis was put up. The Black had left the eggs already.

Dickie had taken food and water and flown twice round the house. He returned to the window, and could not get in. Another bird was looking out at him from behind the trellis. He could see that his mate was not on the nest. He began to call pitifully. No one took any notice.

Squeak investigated the trellis. She knew it already, and knew she could not get through it. She knew also that the air in the other part of the window was of that solid sort which resisted passage. She knew that there was no way out of the loft, nor could the tenants be seen on the patio below. She remained where she was for a while, looking out at the fog. There was a bird outside, calling; it was nothing to do with her. Perhaps the tenants would come out on to the patio, and look up for her.

Meanwhile there was food in the loft. She had eaten at first light, before flying out to find the tenants, but was accustomed at about this hour to dip into a dish of small grains put down for her in the kitchen. She jumped down from the window, and fluttered to the floor to investigate a grain hopper. By the window-wall was an empty home with a nest in it, and in the nest two uncovered eggs. She investigated the eggs, touching them first gently with her beak, then with her chest. They were warm. The memory came to her of eggs, of warm eggs beneath her own body. She sat on the eggs.

When, a couple of hours later, driven by guilt, the other tenant came to the loft to see how Squeak was faring, she was still sitting on the eggs. She took no notice of the tenant at all. The plastic trellis was lifted from the window, Dickie entered, and went at once to the nestbox. In it he found a bird sitting on eggs. He settled by her, and she permitted it. Much later she removed herself from the eggs, and he took her place. She fed, drank, and returned, to couch by his side. Shortly afterwards the flighty Black attempted to enter the nestbox, whereupon Squeak and Dickie set on her together, and drove her out.

There were herself and her mate and their eggs and the home in which they lived. There were other birds of her own kind, but she did not intrude on them, and would not allow them to intrude on her.

There were food and water in places where there had always been food and water, and there was the outside, where one might exercise one's wings, and bathe, and find gravel, or small twigs and straw. Often to be found outside also were two other creatures, sometimes moving, sometimes still, which were harmless in themselves and sometimes a source of hemp or peanuts. One could and should settle on the upper parts of these creatures, because they were extensions of one's own territory, and the claim had to be re-established from time to time. But they were peripheral, not central; they were not truly important. What was important was the protection and hatching of one's eggs, the sharing with one's mate.

There was a disturbance in the loft. One of the

creatures had entered it. They had some connection with the food and water, and could make empty containers full again. The creature moved part of itself towards her.

'Squeakie,' the tenant said. 'You OK, eh?', and extended fingers to her for nibbling.

Squeak looked at the fingers. They were clearly the extrusions of some monstrous animal. She pecked viciously at them, hoping to hurt. She would die to protect her eggs.

Postscript

Much of this story happened, some has been imagined, some rearranged, not much invented. Squeak is alive as I write. Dickie was taken by the hawk (almost certainly not in her presence), and after his death she returned to the tenants for a while, but soon chose another mate. She is an obsessive mother, usually on eggs or feeding youngsters, and therefore spends very little time outside the loft. None of her own eggs has been allowed to hatch, but she has fostered birds of pedigree, and may claim some credit for a number of exceptionally vulgar rosettes.

I have watched her caressing the head of a sick nestling with her beak, tapping its own beak to try to open it, taking the closed beak into her own mouth, grunting and cooing at it in an attempt to persuade it to feed. No other pigeon of the loft, no Chinese Owl or Muffed Tumbler, does as much. She has found her *métier*.